rien ne va plus

rien ne va plus

Margarita Karapanou
translated from the Greek by Karen Emmerich

First published in 2009 by

Clockroot Books
An imprint of Interlink Publishing Group, Inc.
46 Crosby Street, Northampton, Massachusetts 01060
www.clockrootbooks.com

Originally published in Greek by Hermes Publishing in 1991

Library of Congress Cataloging-in-Publication Data
Karapanou, Margarita.
[Rien ne va plus. English]
Rien ne va plus / by Margarita Karapanou ; translated from the Greek by
Karen Emmerich. —1st American ed.
p. cm.
ISBN 978-1-56656-772-5 (pbk.)
I. Emmerich, Karen. II. Title.

PA5622.A696R5413 2009
889'.334—dc22

2009010926

Cover art and design by Ibrie Means

Printed and bound in the United States of America

for my cousin, Constantine

People interpret an action, and each
interpretation is different. Because
in the telling and the retelling, people
reveal not the action, but themselves.
—Akira Kurosawa's *Rashomon*

Demons have faith,
but they tremble.
—Dostoevsky

part one

1.

His eyes were purple, cold, the eyes of a fish. But he was so dazzlingly handsome that his beauty instantly obscured the sense I had of the horror that was to come. All evening, though I found him very attractive, I had the impression that among the guests in the room roamed a reptile with purple eyes, a perfect nose, a handsome mouth, and an exquisite, aggressive sophistication. Alkiviadis talked of nothing but water heaters, how you should leave them off so as not to waste money, and if you do turn them on, it should only be an hour before showering.

—Of course, I always take cold showers, he said, and laughed.

2.

—Why do you suppose I like homosexuality? Alkiviadis asked me.

—Because the people who love you can't ever follow you to the place where you go with the boys. Homosexuality is a hermetically sealed world that belongs to each of us alone. It's almost as if you've died.

Only years later, after the unspeakable had happened, did this statement take on its full significance.

3.

On our wedding night, Alkiviadis suggested we go to a gay bar. I agreed. I still had rice and flowers in my hair.

—I want to show you something, he insisted, flushed and excited, like a child.

I was the only woman in the bar. When I walked in, the men eyed me aggressively, then with curiosity. But when they saw Alkis, they settled down.

—Watch this, he told me.

A blond boy directly across from us was staring at Alkiviadis. He was young, skinny and shy, not even good-looking.

Alkiviadis, who also had rice and flowers in his hair, took a business card from the pocket of the suit he'd worn to the church and went over to the boy. From a distance I listened to his cool, metallic voice, to the insolence barely disguised by his courteous manner.

—My wife and I—we just got married today— would be very pleased if you would come to see us tomorrow evening. Here, the address is on my card, we live in Glyfada. It would make us very happy.

He gave the boy his card. There was something so bizarre about the formality of the scene. My eyes welled with tears. Alkiviadis in his wedding suit, the boy in jeans.

—Well, goodbye, Alkis said.

He came back over to where I was sitting.

—Did you see that? He looked at me.

The boy couldn't have been more than fifteen.

Much later I understood that even then, on the first day of our marriage, Alkiviadis wanted urgently to prove something to me.

—I don't even like him. He lit a cigarette.

There was something so repulsive, yet so seductive about this exchange. I felt as if I'd eaten something I couldn't quite digest right away. It was more than I could deal with, so I erased it from my memory even as it was taking place.

And so on the first night of our marriage I loved Alkiviadis absolutely, as if nothing had happened.

It started to snow. Glyfada went completely white. There were no taxis or buses. Alkiviadis's place didn't have heat. And the water heater was off, so I couldn't even take a hot bath.

—Should I turn it on? I asked.

—No. Go and sit by the space heater.

The snowstorm kept up the next day, too. All day long we made love. Around six Alkiviadis decided to read Proust. He was reading *Le temps retrouvé* when the doorbell rang.

—Who could that be? I asked.

—Must be one of the neighbors. No one would go far in this cold.

I went to answer the door.

The blond boy stood before me, shivering, soaked to the skin.

5

—I walked for hours. Is your husband home?

It occurred to me that I wouldn't have gone out for anyone in such weather. The boy must have wanted Alkis very badly.

I started to shiver, too.

—I'll be right there, Alkiviadis called from the bedroom. Keep him company, I'll be out in a minute.

The boy and I sat down on the sofa. He seemed uncomfortable. I was wearing one of Alkis's sweaters over my nightgown. We were both shivering.

—What sort of work do you do? I asked.

—I'm training to be a flight attendant.

—You like to fly?

—Yes, he said, and smiled, glancing toward the bedroom.

—Would you care for a drink? I'm the lady of the house here, you know.

—Yes. A little brandy, in one of those tall glasses.

His hands were blue from the cold.

—I'm a writer, I told him.

—And I don't really like women, he replied. He took a sip of the brandy and lit a cigarette. This time his smile was twice as wide.

—I can't believe you two got married yesterday.

—Neither can I.

.

Alkis came into the room wearing jeans and a t-shirt. Barefoot. He sat next to the boy and kissed him on the mouth. The boy embraced him so passionately that I understood why he'd walked so far in the snow. It frightened me.

I rose and started toward the bedroom. The cat, Caesar, jumped up on my back as if to strangle me.

Alkiviadis pushed the boy away and chased after me.

—Stay here, he said. It's no fun with just him.

I went back and sat in the armchair. They started kissing again.

—I can't, not with your wife watching.

—But that's what I want, Alkiviadis answered. If you can't, then leave.

They undressed. Their bodies twined together, unbelievably beautiful. I watched, smoking. I liked it. But I still cried.

It's just a bad dream, I thought, *I'll wake up soon.* Then my mind started to wander, as if I really were dreaming, or feverish.

I started to think about my dog Alana. How she sleeps in her very own chair, how she looks at me when she's hungry or wants to be petted, how she rests her head right at the base of my neck as if in prayer. I'd never loved my dog as much as I did on that night with the snow and the moaning, the cold, the two pairs of jeans tossed on the rug.

The boy seemed to feel more at home when they were done.

—Why'd you get married, man? Are you crazy?

Still out of breath, he lit a cigarette and stroked his naked belly. It was the first time he'd spoken to Alkiviadis so informally, using the singular.

—Man, why'd you get married? Are you nuts?

—Get dressed and get out, Alkiviadis snapped. We did what we had to do. Now I want to be with my wife, whom I adore, and to enjoy Proust with her.

—What's Proust?

—A brand of ice cream. Now get up, get dressed, and get out. Just close the door behind you, I don't feel like getting up.

—The jerk went and got married, the boy went on. She's a lucky lady, your wife. She even gets a free show…

—Beat it, or I'll beat you.

Alkis's eyes had gone dark purple, as they always did when he was very angry.

The boy got dressed and left, whistling.

Alkis and I lay down on the bed and began to read Proust.

The answering machine was on, the volume high: *This is Alkiviadis… I'll be back in the office on Monday, January 21st. Until then I'll be away on my honeymoon.* All evening while the blond boy was in the house, and all night after he left, this message kept blaring.

4.

—I love you more than anything, Alkiviadis told me, eyeing the boys around him in the café, who returned his gaze.

    —Alkis, are you only attracted to boys?

    —Yes, but it's you I love.

    My cup of coffee spilled on the lap of the blond boy at the table next to ours. He was wearing green corduroy pants.

    —It's nothing, he said, catching Alkis's eye.

5.

—Do you love me? I asked.
    —More than anything in the world.
    —But you don't love anything.
    —That's why I love you.

6.

—You should be careful, Alkis told me. You're the suicidal type. Depression is a sure road to suicide.

I laughed.

—But Alkis, I could never kill myself. It isn't in my nature, my character; I just don't have it in me. Besides, I find suicide vulgar and aggressive. People only kill themselves in order to hurt other people. It isn't heroic, it's a despicable crime. No, I could never do it. Could you?

Alkis laughed.

—Can you picture me committing suicide?

We both laughed.

—No, I told him. You're the last person in the world who would destroy yourself. You're too narcissistic.

Alkis lit a cigarette, deep in thought. Then he burst out laughing again.

—I'd only kill myself on a weekend, when you were here. For the company.

7.

Alkiviadis was a veterinarian. It was strange, because he didn't like animals. He never petted them. Even my dogs, he'd never petted them, not once.

But during surgery, he handled the animals with infinite tenderness. He was an extraordinary surgeon. I would see such love in his eyes when an animal awoke from anesthesia, an animal he'd saved from death.

It was the same way he looked at me when we'd just made love.

And just as he never touched animals except during surgery, he never touched me unless we were in bed. So, with profound tenderness, I'd come to associate our bed with the operating table.

I never understood Alkiviadis; he was a mystery to the very end. I didn't understand the end, either. But I worshipped Alkis. I was like a dog being taken to the vet, a dog that both worships and fears its doctor. Now, looking back, I see that in the beginning my love for Alkis was very much like the love of a frightened animal in a veterinarian's waiting room.

Alkiviadis once operated on his cat, Caesar. He removed the cat's claws to keep him from ruining the furniture. Like me, Caesar was happy because he loved Alkis. Only one thing scared me: if the cat ever escaped from the house, how would he defend himself against other cats in the street? Me, I let my nails grow.

8.

I watch Caesar jump onto the sofa, the chairs. He scratches at the velvet with his paws. Not a single mark appears, the surfaces remain smooth. Alkis's face, too, remains smooth.

—He doesn't know his claws are gone, so he enjoys it just the same, Alkis says.

Caesar looks quizzically at the sofa and chairs, then down at his feet. He licks his paws and runs to hide under the table. This is the last time I'll see him rush at the furniture with such enthusiasm.

9.

—Alkis, how did you learn to make love like that?

—First with my own body. Then with bodies like mine. And then with you.

—You've never been with another woman? Besides me?

—Sure I have. But they bored me. You don't have to take boys out, or any of that crap. You don't eat in restaurants. You screw. With them it's like being alone. And sex with them isn't at all like making love with a woman.

—What about me?

—You're different. First of all, we're friends, like two men. Besides, I'm in love with you precisely because you're a woman. It's what I always dreamed of. Male bodies bring me closer to you. And you send me back to them.

—Do you still sleep with men?

I was very jealous.

—Now and then.

He laughed.

—No one should have to break his habits.

10.

—I'm a pathological skinflint.

Alkiviadis himself used to tell me this.

—No amount of money could ever be enough. Even if I had a billion dollars it wouldn't be enough, it would seem like nothing. Without money I feel naked, exposed. No matter how much I had, I would still feel that way. Without money I simply don't exist.

—But Alkis, you're incredibly rich.

—And yet I live in a state of panic. I don't like to spend. I like to hoard. Even the sight of an ashtray piled with cigarette butts fills me with satisfaction. When I have to open my wallet to pay for our tickets at the movies my heart pounds, I get dizzy. I didn't want to get married because I didn't want to spend the money. If I could, I'd never leave the house; that way I'd never have to touch my wallet. At night I dream of money. I once dreamed that you were with another man, naked, burning hundreds of thousands, maybe millions of dollars in a fireplace. Afterward the two of you made love in the ashes. I wasn't upset about the other man, just about all that wasted money.

And your little extravagances drive me crazy. It makes me want to throw up every time you buy a pack of cigarettes. Quit smoking, or buy your cigarettes when I'm not around. Don't spend in front of me.

Money is my only passion. That's why I like boys: with them, you don't have to pay for anything.

—Alkiviadis, what is homosexuality?

—To be alone and always to pay for two. But that's when you're old. Me, I've got time.

11.

After we were married, the first thing Alkiviadis did at my place was hang a nylon curtain around my bathtub, with a huge metal bar for support. My bathroom was ruined; it seemed so small and miserable. The curtain was white with pink and purple flowers. Whenever I took a shower, I secretly opened it all the way. And I left the water heater on all the time.

Naturally we received lots of wedding presents. But Alkiviadis wouldn't let me look at them. He put them all in the crawl space. He numbered each one and listed them on a big sheet of paper according to value and size and the guest's reason for buying the gift. He taped the list to the wall and told me:

—We won't ever use them. That way we can send them as gifts whenever we're invited to a wedding or baptism. Why spend money if we don't need to?

—But what about the rocking chair I sent to the island?

—Have it sent back.

One of my aunts had given us a dinner service painted with pale dragons. I liked it. I liked all of the presents, because I loved Alkiviadis. One day Alkis disappeared with the set and didn't come home until evening. He told me he'd spent the whole day going from shop to shop, to all the stores in that chain, trying to exchange the set. And he finally succeeded. He returned home triumphant, carrying a set of white dishes, each with a single yellow butterfly in the center.

—This set is much nicer, he said, and it was cheaper, too, since it has more pieces: there are big plates, little plates, soup bowls, fruit bowls, platters, a gravy boat, even coffee mugs.

—But I don't like it, I said.

He lit a cigarette and started to read. Then he raised his head and looked at me, smiling.

—*Rien ne va plus*, he said.

—Isn't that what they say in roulette?

—Yes. It's not as ominous as it sounds. But it marks the most crucial moment of the game. That's what gives it that terseness, that sense of conclusion.

—What exactly does it mean?

—It's the moment when you can't affect the future anymore, for better or worse. When you hear the croupier's famous *Rien ne va plus*, you either win or lose whatever you've bet. Usually you lose.

—But sometimes you win, I insisted.

—Hardly ever. Roulette is a deadly game.

12.

After we were married, Alkiviadis decided that we would continue to live separately, each in our own apartment. We would only see each other on weekends, at Alkis's place. But going to visit my own husband at his house every weekend proved as difficult as arranging an adulterous affair. I had to leave my dogs with a friend, pack a suitcase, lower the blinds, and turn off the water heater—Alkis insisted on that. He lived in Glyfada. I remember the busy avenue, the hideous glass buildings, the ugliness, the thousands of cars, the noise, the cab drivers' curses... I always arrived hungry.

—Tonight I have a delicious meal planned for you, Alkiviadis would tell me. Bulgur and tomatoes.

I was always very hungry, and I liked whatever Alkiviadis made, because I loved him. And because after the bulgur and tomatoes we would fall into bed for two days, and the water heaters, the ugly dishes, the aggravation of the trip there, all dissolved into pleasure.

After we were married, Alkiviadis told me:

—I need days when I can be alone, to think, to day-dream.

—But you're alone all week long, I answered.

—Yes, but even on weekends, when you come, I still want a few hours to myself.

—I spend half of every weekend at your house writing, I answered. You have least fifteen hours to yourself.

—I get jealous when you write. You don't belong to me anymore. I want you to read. And I'll choose the book. A book that won't excite you, that won't make me jealous. How about *The Three Musketeers*?

—I've already read it.

—Read it again.

13.

Once while Alkis was stroking me and kissing my hips, there in the small hollow just below my waist, he said:
 —You're so handsome.
 —Beautiful, you mean.
 —No. Handsome. You have the hips of a little boy. I adore you.
 That aroused me. We made love, and the whole time I felt like a woman in a boy's body and with a boy's soul. From then on we always made love that way, starting with a kiss on my hip.

14.

—Alkis, look how handsome that man is!

—Mmmm… not bad. Especially his stomach, with that narrow waist.

I became his accomplice. Afterward, alone in my apartment, I'd fall to the floor and howl like a dog. So as not to kill him. Because I liked it. I became his ally in this ritual of the gaze. I pointed out boys to him all the time. It became an obsession for me, like constantly checking my watch though I already knew the time. And I trembled under their stares. Alkiviadis was the one they wanted, through my gaze, and I offered him up to them every time. We were always seeking each other out with our eyes, always, everywhere, every moment of the day and night—especially at night. One of us watched another who watched yet another. These looks were sensuous, pleasureful, they had nothing to do with the deadly hatred of desire. An exquisite combination that plunged me deeper every day into an exquisite hell. These gazes concealed a sanctuary: the sanctuary of my own soul, which became more and more aroused by what it hated most. And so hate and pleasure became one. And I, nothing at all.

part one

15.

Alkiviadis and I were nothing alike. We were opposites
in everything. I spent money left and right, said whatever came into my head, would laugh or cry at the drop
of a hat, and got up at five in the morning. Generally
speaking, I was impossible, but in a sweet, harmless way.

—That's why I married you, Alkiviadis used to say.
Because you're a lovely, impossible madwoman.

Our meetings seemed almost hieratic, since they
were absolutely fixed in place and time: Alkis's apartment, every Saturday. Once I lost track of what day it
was and went a day early, on Friday. I realized my mistake just as the taxi was pulling up in front of his house,
and it seemed like such a crime that I told the driver to
take me back home. That was when I first began to love
Alkiviadis less.

Another time I went on the right day, but an hour
early, to surprise him. Alkiviadis was furious; we fought
as we'd never fought before. He kept shouting over and
over:

—I have to be completely psychologically prepared
if I'm going to see you. Don't ever do that again. Ever.

Me, I just cried. I looked out the window and cried,
because I didn't understand why what I had done was so
wrong.

16.

—Alkis, I had a dream. Do you want to hear?

   —Sure.

   —My cousin Alexander is sleeping. He's been awake for years, but today, all of a sudden, he decided to sleep. He lay down, crossed his hands on his chest, and curled himself into a ball so he could drop into the well of sleep: he had to take on a shape that could attain the necessary depth and speed—that's what he told me, anyway.

   He gathered his clothes into little mounds— sweaters, pants, shirts. He put them in suitcases and locked them up.

   I'll find them here when I wake up, he told me conspiratorially.

   He lay down, closed his eyes, and fell asleep.

   Now I'm watching from a hilltop as he falls peacefully into the well. Thousands of mirrors are watching him, and no matter how far he falls, the well keeps getting deeper, because the well is entirely his own—he explained it all to me.

   There are strange shapes scrawled on the walls.

   I remember them, he told me, from dreams I had when I was a baby, but I have to sleep very deeply if I want to have those dreams again. Jungles, animals with green wings, beautiful monsters—he pointed them out to me as he fell.

From the hilltop where I'm standing I watch him falling slowly, and the mouth of the well seems to be climbing into the sky. Then a cloud passes directly overhead and covers it up.

Alexander is falling slowly, now he's almost at the center of the earth—I can see him clearly from the hilltop. I can see the other side of the earth, too, and I'm waiting. My cousin hovers there for a while, exactly in the center of the earth, and it's as if the earth is widening at exactly that spot, like a smile. As he falls and comes out the other side I start to run, I circle the whole earth to catch up with him.

My cousin starts moving faster, until he's falling like a meteorite. A million years passed in an instant, I saw the center of the earth close up again, a million years passed and I watch him from the hilltop, falling, drunken, happy, forever.

—Go to sleep, Alkiviadis said. Go to sleep. Don't wake me up again. My sleep is sacred, you know that. I have to be at work early in the morning. Keep your dreams to yourself. They have nothing to do with me.

17.

Alkis and I went to see Bergman's *Fanny and Alexander*. In the movie there's a horrible bishop who torments his wife and her children. As we left the theater I said to Alkiviadis:

—The bishop reminds me of you. I hereby baptize you the Bishop, that's what I'm going to call you from now on. That's just how you torment me, and if we had kids you'd torment them too.

So I stopped calling him Alkis. And how I longed to go back to my childhood home, like the woman in the movie! Each weekend I went to Glyfada with increasing unease. I didn't want to see the Bishop anymore. At some point, on one of our weekends together, he was sure to do something terrible.

—Alkis, I don't want to come to your place anymore.

—It seems to me... Alkis said.

He started every one of his sentences with that unbearable, pompous "it seems to me."

—It seems to me that you didn't understand the movie at all. The bishop torments the children for their own good. It's a sort of initiation, to help them grow up. That's why he torments his wife, too. And deep down, his wife adores him. If she hated him, Bergman wouldn't have made the movie. It wouldn't have been the least bit interesting. If his wife didn't love him, why would she go and live with him?

—But she runs away.

—Yes, Alkiviadis replied, because she longs for her childhood, her house, and her mother, who's the symbol of comfort and ease. The fact that she goes back home is a sign of failure. She couldn't bear to grow up. The harshness, even the cruelty, it's all part of becoming an adult. The bishop shows her life as it really is, and it isn't the dream she'd prefer to go on living.

I was furious.

—Is that why you pulled out Caesar's claws? To help him grow up? You're the fool, Alkis, you're the one who didn't understand the movie. The wife is the real adult. The bishop is the immature one, since he needs to be inhuman in order to exist. And his wife doesn't "go back," as you say. She returns to where she belongs, to maturity.

—You didn't understand at all, Alkiviadis insisted.

The battle raged all night. Never before had we spoken so heatedly, never before had he tried so passionately to convince me of anything. Because in talking about the movie, we were really talking about our marriage. Alkiviadis understood this. I, however, did not.

The next weekend I went out and rented some movies, stretched out with my dogs on my own bed in my own home, and whispered:

—I'll never go to see the Bishop again.

18.

Alkiviadis and I went to Paris. One afternoon when he had gone off on his own I went shopping with Christina, a childhood friend, and then went back to her place. We laughed at our purchases, all these things we'd never wear. Then we decided to watch *Jaws*. We'd seen it five times together and countless times apart. Christina liked to be scared, but only by movies. We tried on our new blouses again.

—I'll never wear this, it's too nice, Christina said.

—Why don't you get highlights? I asked.

—What are you talking about? My hair is full of highlights, can't you tell? she asked, upset.

—Oh, Christina, I wish this day would never end. Let's stay like this forever, talking about highlights and clothes.

—Are you on a diet? she asked.

—A great one, I answered. You eat nothing but raisins soaked in brandy, so you're always drunk and your appetite just disappears.

We laughed. Time passed. It was a quarter past eight. We were watching *Jaws*, squeezing our eyes shut during the scene when the shark bites the girl in half in the water. We always shut our eyes during that scene, so we'd still never seen it.

Now it was half past nine.

—What happened to Alkiviadis? Christina suddenly asked.

I was embarrassed.

—Let's eat. Something must have come up.

Just then the doorbell rang. Alkiviadis came in, flushed. He barely even said hello.

—Come into the bathroom, he said to me.

—But we're about to eat, I said.

—Come into the bathroom.

Alkiviadis, usually so formal and polite, was treating me incredibly rudely.

In the bathroom, Alkiviadis sat on the lid of the toilet. He took me in his arms and began to speak in a monotone, as if lulling me to sleep.

—The two of us share everything. Everything. Well, I went to a gay porn theater. I bought a ticket at the door. The room was dark, and there was hard-core porn on the screen. At first I couldn't see anything, but after a while I began to make out the figures of boys walking around. The room was all aisles, and there were boys climbing up to the balcony and down to the restrooms, circling the seats, which were all empty: no one was watching the movie, everyone was milling around like shadows, lit up only by the screen. I felt as if I were dreaming. Then I started to walk with them. Our bodies brushed against one another in the dark, and the contact was like a rustling, like souls touching. The boys were like sleepwalkers, tiptoeing around. No one spoke. We walked like that for hours, as if pacing the perimeter of a prison yard. We looked at one another, but we couldn't make out any faces in the dark, or didn't want to. Only the bodies, the bodies, the hips, the backs. Hands stroked my face and I stroked others. We were like blind men, condemned to walk in circles forever.

One boy stood in front of the screen. I could see him clearly. He was very handsome, kind of wild, with a gold ring in one ear. He was smoking, and his head made a black stain on the screen. His earring was perfectly visible. There were two men on the screen.

Fuck me, you bastard! Fuck me! one was shouting to the other.

But the things happening on the screen were wild and savage, while the atmosphere in the room was oddly sweet, like an unfamiliar wine.

We wandered like that for hours. Then suddenly we climbed up onto the balcony.

Now the couples changed at a frightening pace. I must have had twenty or thirty boys, and ten or twenty more had me.

We clung to one another like grapes. One man's breath would ripple out, becoming a source of pleasure for us all. We went wild. I bit the boy with the earring, hard, and sucked at his blood. If we hadn't stopped when we did, we all would've died. At some point I found a door and pushed my way out onto the street. I ran off.

That night I dreamed of Dante's Inferno. It was full of boys and bathrooms, and an angel with hair down to his waist kept flushing the toilets.

19.

Alkiviadis and I divorced hurriedly, nervously, the same way we'd married.

I didn't see him for two years.

Sometime in the spring, I received a prize in Paris for the best foreign novel. I had a party at my place and got flowers and telegrams from all over the world.

It was five in the morning when I heard Alkis's voice on the answering machine.

—Congratulations, little monster. It seems to me that this calls for a celebration.

I hadn't heard his voice in two years. It sounded different, but I couldn't put my finger on the change. Then it hit me: his voice was warm and open, so unlike his old, distant haughtiness.

The doorbell rang before I had time to get completely dressed. I opened the door and saw Alkiviadis standing before me. He was so handsome, his manner so changed that I couldn't bear it and closed my eyes. When I opened them again he was still standing there, glowing. The harsh lines around his mouth had disappeared. In the past, his smile always used to twist into a grimace, but now he was smiling sweetly. He had always been handsome, but now he was blindingly so, since there was no harshness or pettiness about him anymore. He looked so brilliant, so magnificent, that I remember putting a hand to my chest, feeling as if my ribcage would burst and my heart would plunge to the floor. He'd lost a lot of weight. His purple eyes were huge. And his hair was longer. His face drank me in, consumed me. He folded me in his arms.

—Congratulations, my little Proust.

He was holding an enormous bouquet of red roses. He looked at the flower arrangements that covered every surface in the room.

—They've sent you white roses, yellow, pink. I'm glad to see no one has sent you red.

We went to a bar. As we clinked glasses I laughed happily and asked:

—So what are we celebrating?

—Your award, of course. He looked thoughtfully out the window and lit a cigarette.

Then, suddenly, he grabbed my wrist.

—We're celebrating other things, too, he said. First of all, the fact that I haven't seen you in two years, and now we're going to spend the night together.

He squeezed my wrist tightly and I began to sweat, from fear, just as in the old days. Was it the lighting in the bar, or had his face lost the peace and calm I had seen at my place just a short while before? The bar was completely empty. Our table was in a corner. The two of us were sitting like statues on a stage, seconds before the curtain was to rise.

—I'm working on something fairly big myself, Alkis told me.

I knew he had been doing veterinary research.

—Something unique, he continued, that has nothing to do with my work. So we're celebrating that, too. That, and our night together.

—And my award, I said.

He didn't answer. Again, he looked thoughtfully out the window.

At my place we made love. Afterward, stretched out on his back, Alkiviadis smoked a cigarillo.

—You must have missed me these two years, whether you know it or not. You must've missed it all, he said. You may have hated it, but you liked it, too. You divorced me out of fear, precisely because you liked it.

In the morning, he smiled at me as he left.

—Will I see you again? I asked.

—From now on, you'll be seeing me all the time.

I fell asleep. When I awoke, something was bothering me. I replayed my night with Alkiviadis over and over in my mind, as if it were a chess game. After two years without contact, there was something unfinished, something impenetrable about our single night together. Something important had escaped me, but it was hiding in some detail that I couldn't pin down. Was it some gesture, some expression, some phrase Alkis had used? This bizarre chess game played itself out incessantly in my mind, and I couldn't give it an end. I had the white pieces, but on the other side of the board, the black king was missing, as if it had withdrawn from the game, no longer desiring a confrontation.

That afternoon I started calling Alkiviadis. At the office, at home. It was five. He was always at the office at five. But the answering machine didn't even pick up. No one picked up anywhere.

At six I called his apartment again. An unfamiliar voice answered.

—Sorry, I must have dialed the wrong number.

I hung up and dialed again. The same voice answered.

—Sorry, the lines must be crossed.

I hung up and dialed again.

—Is this Alkiviadis's house?

—Yes. May I ask who's calling?

—I'm his ex-wife. Who are you?

—I'm with the police.

—Alkiviadis… it's a car accident, isn't it?

—No, he answered.

We were both silent.

I heard the man light a cigarette and inhale.

—Your ex-husband committed suicide. He's dead.

I heard a scream sweeping through the room, over the furniture, the curtains. It was coming from me.

—Please come right away. We're expecting you. His family is here. We're looking for some papers of his.

Again, after two years, I took a cab through those same streets, with the same ugly buildings, the traffic, the noise, the shop windows full of bridal gowns. Though I didn't quite know it then, as I stood in front of the building where he'd lived, a mechanism of hate and survival had already been set in motion inside of me. For the first time I noticed how shabby and depressing his building was. Now, whenever I close my eyes, that building appears before me, nameless, unmentionable.

The apartment was crowded, a tangle of relatives and policemen. The only person crying was one of the officers.

—I have a son the same age. Handsome, too, just like him.

Alkis's father was lying face-down on the floor, his arms crossed.

—Son, why did you do this to us? What did we do wrong? Speak to me, son, speak to me.

His mother was sitting like a mummy in one of the chairs. She wasn't crying. She didn't even blink. Whenever anyone came up to comfort her she would push them away.

—I should've given him his blue sweater before they took him away, she said in a calm, steady voice. The light blue one he loved so much.

Everyone was looking for his papers. Driver's license, identification card, passport. They couldn't find them anywhere.

—I know where they are, I said. I found them in a second. No one could have guessed that Alkis kept his ID tucked into the Book of Revelation, his passport in *À la recherche du temps perdu*, and his driver's license in an empty cat food can.

—Thank you so much, said one of the officers. He couldn't have been buried without these.

—Will there be a service, even though he committed suicide? I asked.

—We'll take care of that, the officer replied.

Alkis's apartment, which he had always kept so clean, was filthy. The kitchen was strewn with the broken shards of dirty dishes. The floor was covered with pasta that was several days old. You couldn't walk without slipping in grease. It smelled unbearably foul. Only when I saw that kitchen, which I remembered as glisteningly clean, was I finally able to cry.

I went into his bedroom and closed the door. The room was a mess. The same old sheets on the bed, white with purple flowers. We'd made love so many times on those sheets, we'd fought, we'd laughed. Now they were buried under a mountain of pills that spilled onto the floor. You could hardly see carpet. There were glasses everywhere, half filled with brandy. Blood on the sheets. Dirty clothes piled haphazardly on the floor. He who had always been so clean. On the bed, the hollow where his body had been just a half-hour before. I lay down in that hollow. It was still warm. I fell asleep. I could faintly hear the officers conducting their investigations; they even unscrewed the pipes in the bathroom—"You think there are drugs?" I heard one of them ask. Alkiviadis's aunt was in there, too, brushing her cheeks with rouge.

Suddenly I remembered how Alkis used to keep notes about his affairs with the boys: *With so-and-so we went first out for a drink, and afterward I threw him out fast...*

I didn't want anyone to find those notes. I went straight to his Bible. Fortunately he'd only written on one page, but it was big and thick, and covered in details. I chewed it up and swallowed it bit by bit. I almost choked. The police had cut off the water. I went into the kitchen to make coffee with bottled water. Now all the relatives were crying—and it was so funny—I

ground the beans—Alkis always bought whole beans—
and the machine made a deafening noise. Everyone was
staring at me.

—Just a dizzy spell, I told them.

Alkiviadis's mother looked at me.

—We'll be taking Caesar home with us, she said.
We can let him out in the yard.

I thought again about how Caesar hadn't had any
claws since the procedure Alkiviadis had performed.
How would he defend himself against the other cats in
the neighborhood, not to mention a dog? If Alkiviadis
had known back then that he was going to kill himself,
would he have removed the cat's claws? That question
will always torment me, even more than his suicide.

I lay down again in the hollow on the bed where his
body had been only a short while before and began to
chant out loud, like a liturgy:

—May you be cursed where you're going, too, for
all of eternity.

May you be cursed and condemned to live in a hell
without boys.

I fell asleep. I dreamed of my dog Lyn, who had been
poisoned the previous year on the island.

Lyn was the only dog I ever really adored. I'd had
dogs ever since I was little, but Lyn was the only one I

loved completely, absolutely. She was small, fragile, kind of stupid. But that lack of intelligence may have been what made me love her the way I did. She was so defenseless. I always wondered what she would do if some cat attacked her, since she didn't know how to fight. She was so beautiful, with her golden fur! She was always a little frightened, always clinging to my legs. And she adored me, too. Our relationship was like that of a mother and daughter, when the daughter refuses to grow up and the mother steadfastly offers an ambiguous love, a complicity, in order to keep her daughter close.

Lyn had a blue ball that played "The Blue Danube" when she chewed on it. She never did, though, because she didn't want to ruin it. She always took it with her when we went to the beach. She was very proud of that ball. She never went in the water. She sat on my towel, and I would put a little hat on her, with green and purple flowers. Lyn was the baby Alkis had never given me. He often told me how much he hated children, mostly on the days when I could've gotten pregnant, when I would beg him, "Alkis, please, give me a child," and he would say to me, "I detest children," and take all the necessary precautions so I wouldn't get pregnant. After my swim Lyn would wait patiently until it was time for us to go home. She never expressed her desires, the way other dogs do. I always had to guess what she wanted. I suppose it amused her. And she was capricious, even with her food. She would circle her bowl several times, look at me slyly, run into the yard and come back with a cicada in her mouth, then pick at her food as if she couldn't stand the sight of it. Sometimes she wouldn't eat at all.

But one morning, out in the yard, she ate a pellet of rat poison that was hidden inside a lump of freshly ground meat. Lyn was crazy about ground meat. That happened on a Monday afternoon at twenty-five past four. From when she swallowed the poison until the moment she died, the next morning, exactly at nine—I remember the time, because as she was dying in my arms the bells in the island's bell tower rang exactly nine times—the blood slowly emptied out of her body, and it seemed as if the sky were raining blood, as if the whole island had been flooded with blood and had turned bright red, lashed by some unearthly rain. Instead of urine, blood flowed from her constantly, until it flooded my room. But she was on her best behavior, right to the very end. Lyn never whimpered, never cried. Perhaps she wasn't in pain, I don't know. Though deep down I knew she was in terrible pain, because she'd be stricken by spasm and her eyes would fill with panic. I wanted to believe that she wasn't in pain, because otherwise I wouldn't have been able to bear it, but really I knew that she was suffering indescribably. She was so well behaved that in the beginning, so as not to soil the room, she would jump down and go to the newspaper I had spread out for her on the floor, and when she had finished she would jump back onto the bed and curl up in my arms. Later that night when the real hemorrhaging began, when the newspaper was completely soaked and she was no longer strong enough to reach it, she just let her blood spill out everywhere. Dark purple rivulets of blood ran across the floor, my bedroom smelled like a slaughterhouse. Between each of these discharges I would hug her, lift her carefully and lay her down on the bed, where she would cuddle against my neck. "Lyn," I would say, "Lyn." My sheets, too, became soaked with blood. I looked at the moon. It was a full moon, blood-red, huge and threatening.

Her death, or rather her murder, lasted all night long. With poison you don't die right away the way Alkis did when he took the pills he used to put dogs to sleep. He died instantaneously. The poison Lyn ate tears up the intestines, but doesn't affect the heart or any of the other organs right away. Whereas Alkis, the veterinarian, knew exactly what he was doing. With the pills he took you die for sure, and instantaneously. How much I hated him for that! Why did Lyn, who wanted to live, have to suffer, and not Alkis, who wanted to die? How much I hated him, in my dream, as I lay in the hollow on his bed, which was still warm from his body.

It took Lyn twelve hours to die. Alkis died within minutes.

Something that still bothers me even now, just like the thought of Alkis's cat Caesar—who, if he'd had his claws, could have protected himself if he ever got out of the house—is this: if Lyn had eaten her food on the day she died, the afternoon of Monday, August 30th, would she have eaten the poison, too? Or would she have been full and not even have touched the meat?

In the morning, as the end drew near, I hugged her with all my strength. I was crying.

—Lyn, the place you're going won't be so bad. In paradise you'll have other dogs to play with. Everyone says paradise is a nice place. Just don't be afraid of the big dogs, and make sure to eat well. There are green hills there, and fresh, sweet-smelling earth to dig holes in, and you love doing that. And I bet there's no sea, the sea you hate.

Lyn died in my arms on Tuesday morning, exactly at nine. I buried her in the yard, put a pretty piece of marble and a wooden cross on the grave, and planted red bougainvillea around it.

Then I lay down in the hollow on my bed, which was still warm from her body, and began to chant out loud, like a liturgy:

—May you be blessed, where you're going, for all of eternity.

May you be blessed, may you live in a paradise full of trees and fresh earth, greenery, and lots of dogs.

Later, I took a bucket and mop and cleaned up the blood.

20.

—Alkis, you never gave me anything. You've only taken. In death as in life.

Even now that you're dead, you still eat away at me, more and more, insatiably.

I'm stupid, I let you do it. But you're stupid, too. You don't realize that by eating me you're poisoning yourself, and that even in hell, poison can still give you stomach cramps and nausea.

What first attracted me to you, when I met you and fell in love, is what repels me now: your deep, metaphysical indifference to everything and everyone—most of all to yourself, to the universe, and to God.

That's why you killed yourself. Because you couldn't fear a God you don't believe in, but who exists, whether you like it or not. And for God, there's no hubris worse than suicide. He created you, and only he has the right to decide when to call you back to his side.

The only person you were ever interested in was yourself. Whenever you treated anyone else with love, it was only so you could collect interest on that debt later. You never acted with any real generosity. Kindness is easy, as you know perfectly well. Because with kindness, you're not really giving anything.

I'm talking about giving your soul to your fellow human beings—and not just to the ones you love. I'm

44

talking about compassion. Compassion means "to suffer with": to suffer because someone else is suffering, to endure *with* the other, or in *place* of the other. You have no idea what that even means. It was all foreign to you while you were alive, and must be even more so now that you're dead. Wherever you are, I hope you're listening. Now that you're dead I can finally speak my mind, because I'm not afraid of you anymore.

You always functioned as a mirror for others; you changed according to what each person wanted from you. But you always came up short, your whole life. After all, we can never really know other people's true intentions or desires, which even they can't know for sure. And with your suicide you blew it again, because you were so quickly forgotten. It's human nature to forget, especially the unpleasant things.

There isn't a single flower on your grave anymore. Only dust and ants.

I think a lot about your cat Caesar, much more than I think about you. Since you must have known you would kill yourself one day, why did you pull out his claws, when you knew that without his claws he wouldn't be able to defend himself? That thought haunts me more than any other, much more than the thought of your suicide, which was your own affair, after all, something you chose. But the cat wanted his nails, he didn't choose to have them removed, you chose for him—and I can never forgive you for that, do you hear me? Never.

For as long as we lived together, I was always the one who gave. You took and took and took, though you always told me you loved me. That's why I stopped loving you, long before you died. But you never even realized, because you never paid attention to anyone but yourself. Alkis, I stopped loving you because I was tired. And I got tired because you never really paid any attention to me. I was only your mirror. You never gave me anything. But since you never paid any attention to me, you never understood how tired I was.

You were always telling me, "I give to you, I give you everything." But you never gave me anything. I can't remember a single thing you've ever given me, other than exhaustion—and that exhaustion came in perfect doses, just enough so I wouldn't be completely destroyed, and would stay with you for exactly as long as you needed me.

Alkis, I still love you, a little. For fleeting moments. But most of the time I hate you. As much as you hated me while you were alive, maybe even more.

Alkis, the marble of your gravestone is cold. I press my cheek against it and listen to make sure you're not still alive. I haven't stopped being afraid of you. I'm even more afraid of you now that you're dead than I was when you were alive, because now you can sneak in any-where, invisibly.

Alkis, don't ever hurt me again. You'll end up getting poisoned, just like before.

part two

21.

God says:
Man has places in his heart that don't yet exist. Pain
permeates them, and brings them into existence.

22.

The game starts again from the beginning. The end is always another beginning.
    This nightmare of eternity in time, this is our fate.

23.

Eros is diabolical: it constantly withholds what it promises, and constantly promises what it intends to withhold.

24.

This small thing, a movement, something particular but not significant, which nevertheless changes everything, and creates the Singular.

25.

This hour, at the end of the day. Silence.

26.

What can I say? And why should I say anything? I'll never speak again, I'll sew up my mouth with a golden needle and golden thread.

My tongue sticks in my throat, and slowly I swallow it.

My soul has moved, I can't find it anymore.

I don't care.

27.

Joy is the same thing as pain, the same thing as death.

But death, is it joy?

28.

Moments of hopelessness should always be transformed
into creation.

But why?
    And for whom?

Essentially, creation is always boring, since it's an eter-
nal lie—otherwise it can never become Art. And the lie
is boring, too, since it has no real effect.

29.

To forget is the great secret of strong people.

To remember, to rehash, is the worst of human weaknesses, one for which others always pay.

Though of course you, too, always pay.

part two

30.

My God, so distant and close:
    —If I come to hate you, it will mean I have finally
begun to believe in You.

31.

Lord, who have built our way to the skies, who have transformed destruction into salvation, listen…

32.

And God speaks:
    I am the Way, the Truth, and the Life:
    No one comes to God the Father except through
me, because I am God the Father.

33.

The end has arrived.
   But not even that can release me.
   Because there is no End.

                         Amen.

part three

34.

His eyes were purple, warm, friendly. He was so handsome that his good looks kept you from seeing how
pleasant and agreeable he was. His name was Alkiviadis.
I met him one Saturday at Aunt Louisa's. She owned a
huge estate in Ekali, just north of Athens, where she
lived with her twenty-seven dogs, lots of canaries, a parrot, fish, children, grandchildren, and her husband Miltos. Aunt Louisa had built an earthly paradise around
her. Though really it was Aunt Louisa who gave that
taste of paradise to her surroundings. I went to see them
every Saturday. As soon as I opened the gate a crowd of
dogs, large and small, would come running to greet me,
and I'd hear the chattering of birds from the house, and
Aunt Louisa would rush outside, smiling, her arms
flung wide, lapdogs yapping at her skirts. An infinite
happiness would wash over me. It was a virgin house, a
house that had never been touched by anything bad; as
soon as you set foot on the property you felt as if you'd
been doused with some cool, magic elixir.

It wasn't just chance that I met Alkiviadis there.

That Saturday we sat, as always, in the living room.
How well I remember Alkiviadis, in a large armchair to
my right, stroking the little white dog in his lap.

—He's a veterinarian, Aunt Louisa told me proudly.
The best. We all just adore him. He's the son of a close

friend. You've never met him before because he doesn't usually come on Saturdays.

—Today I was lucky. Alkiviadis smiled at me.

Me too, I thought, then blushed as if I'd said it out loud.

Aunt Louisa and Uncle Miltos went outside to feed the German shepherds.

Alkis and I were alone. But there wasn't a single awkward moment between us. He smoked an entire cigarette before either of us said a word, though we were both smiling—perhaps because we could hear Aunt Louisa yelling, "Miltos! Wolf ate all of Valdis's food!"

As we sat there silently grinning, I suddenly thought, *It's as if we're in our own home.* I blushed again, embarrassed. The thought was absurd; Alkis and I had barely even spoken.

—I like coming here, Alkis said. I leave feeling so invigorated. I can't explain it, it's like…

—I know, I said, and laughed. I know.

He stood up.

—Let's go upstairs to see the birds. If your aunt keeps on collecting them at this rate, before long the house will be a jungle. You know, he continued, you have beautiful eyes.

We were separated by a large pink cage. Our eyes met through the fluttering wings of canaries. There were dozens of cages in the room, and the chattering of the birds was deafening. The walls were lined with aquariums where fish swam in silent circles among seaweed and rocks. The parrot kept screeching, "Down with the right!"

The whole room seemed to be fluttering. Sunlight streamed through the large windows, tingeing the birds, the cages, and the aquariums with gold, making Alkis's purple eyes look incredibly beautiful. *This is paradise*, I thought. *Let this moment last forever, just like this, that's all I want.*

Months later, when I told Alkis that the love we shared was something rare, he answered:

—Just wait. This is only the beginning.

On that first Saturday, thinking about paradise and listening to the high, clear cries of the canaries, I had only a foretaste of paradise. I experienced the real paradise later on, with Alkis. I think our first meeting at Aunt Louisa's was decisive. That day, everything conspired to bring us together. Love is white magic, and all around us that magic was at work. Perhaps elsewhere it never would have happened.

We went back down to the living room, and Alkis sat in the same chair. I sat a bit closer to him than before, at the edge of the sofa.

—I adore animals, he told me. I have ever since I was a kid. I feel compassion for them, since even the wildest ones are defenseless before humans. And that compassion grows even stronger when sick animals come into my office. I lift them onto the table and before I ever touch them I speak to them gently and they relax, just as a human would, because they understand that they're there for their own good. When I can't save an animal and it dies, I'm sick for days. I have a cat, you know. His name is Caesar. You'll meet him.

—I have two dogs.

—Will I meet them?

—Of course.

The rest of the family trickled in. Aunt Louisa, Uncle Miltos, my cousin with her husband and three sons, my other cousin and his wife. They all lived in different houses on the estate and gathered each night at Aunt Louisa's for dinner. There wasn't room for us all at the table and we were laughing and the kids were shouting, "Ice cream! Ice cream!"

—Quiet! I'm trying to listen to the news on TV! Uncle Miltos yelled.

—Vanilla or chocolate? Aunt Louisa called from the kitchen.

—I want to watch a movie! A movie with murders! cried one of my nephews.

Alkis and I laughed so hard that tears ran from our

eyes. He came and sat beside me on the sofa. The whole house had become one huge buzz, like a beehive. The canaries, the parrot—which was now screeching "I am the General!"—the commercials on TV, the kids, Aunt Louisa telling a story that no one could hear.

But within that pandemonium a secret, silent circle was forming around Alkis and me. We were like two fish in an aquarium, silently seeking each other out, swimming toward one another very fast, without looking at one another, without touching. Much later Alkis told me he had felt exactly the same thing right then, like telepathy. We didn't know then that those moments during our first encounter at Aunt Louisa's were to change our lives.

I watched Aunt Louisa. She was short and plump, with the most beautiful smile I had ever seen. When she smiled, her whole face lit up, and her body, too. And she was almost always smiling. She was smart, but she was also good—a rare combination. She wasn't exactly an eccentric, but she had all the humor and charm of a person with imagination. Aunt Louisa loved everyone and everything, and respected all living things, people and animals alike. She had an inexhaustible well of energy, which was contagious, too, and everyone adored her for that. She gave unstintingly and never expected anything in return. She told incredible stories—or rather, the way she told them was incredible: she would get one tangled up in another, so that the simplest incident would become a *Thousand and One Nights*. Her stories didn't make much sense, but I could sit and listen to her for ages. I liked to watch her fling her arms wide or imitate different people, standing up and sitting back down to give emphasis to her words. She was always surrounded by a cloud of little lapdogs. They burrowed in her skirts, perched on her shoulders, stretched out at her feet—I had never seen her without them. Sometimes the dogs would create the illusion of a colorful fur coat fluttering over her dress. I adored Aunt Louisa. I always sat next to her, hoping to absorb some of her energy and love.

—The dog didn't have leptospirosis, there was nothing wrong with it at all, the vet was a fool, he had no idea what he was talking about. How many vets have we gone through, Miltos, a dozen? And Alkis doesn't want to be our vet, since he'd have to come all this way—how could we possibly get twenty-seven dogs to his office?

Alkiviadis laughed.

—But Louisa, I'd have to close my practice, I'd have to move in here and be your personal veterinarian, like in the nineteenth century when royal courts had their own doctors. He winked at her. Actually, Louisa, I like the idea. I'd get to stay forever in paradise. Alkis sighed, and murmured, Outside this house, real life is waiting.

Then he turned and looked at me. He looked me deep in the eyes. It was the first time he had revealed himself to me in that way, and his gaze held something like a promise.

—But I guess each of us has to make his own paradise.

We didn't know it at the time, but later we would both realize that with this sentence, Alkiviadis had proposed to me.

That night we ate the strangest assortment of foods. Pasta, pork, chicken, sausage, fresh fruit and preserves, which Louisa set out on the table before the main dishes were ready—it was all jumbled together on the table, main dishes, ice cream and sweets. The kids dumped ice cream on top of their meat, there was a kung fu movie playing, Aunt Louisa's dogs were all barking, and the parrot shrilled, "Moron! Moron!" The canaries flew and chattered in their cages, making a racket.

Alkis, seated across from me, was smiling a secretive smile. He wasn't looking at me, but I could feel his presence, as his exquisite hands, a surgeon's hands, crumbled a piece of bread. And all the while the love that flooded the house was bringing us closer and closer together.

Aunt Louisa was describing a movie she'd seen:

—The mother bear and her cub were always together, it followed her everywhere. Miltos, would you give me some sauce, and children, don't shout—so her baby just followed her everywhere, Miltos, why don't we get a bear cub?

It was eleven o'clock.

—I'm going out to put up the German shepherds, Uncle Miltos announced.

—Really, how do you deal with all those German shepherds? Alkis asked. Don't they fight with the other male dogs?

Uncle Miltos sat back down and lit a cigarette.

—My dear Alkis, it's quite simple. All the big dogs live outside in huge kennels, like houses. I've even installed central heating. I let the German shepherds and the setters out at different times, I've developed a system, it's really quite simple. The only problem is that I can't ever travel. Louisa and I dream of going to Switzerland, where we went for our honeymoon, but it's impossible. Who would take care of the dogs? If someone made a mistake and let the setters and German shepherds out at the same time, they'd eat one another alive.

—Tell me how it works, and I'll decide for myself how simple it is.

—Well, my system operates on a twenty-four-hour basis. I let the German shepherds out from one to eight every morning. At eight I lock them up and let out the setters. At ten-thirty I lock up the setters and let out the German shepherds. At one in the afternoon I lock up the German shepherds and let out the setters. At five I lock up the setters and let out the German shepherds. At seven I lock up the German shepherds and let out the setters. At nine I lock up the setters and let out the German shepherds. At eleven I lock up the German shepherds and let out the setters. One a.m., lock up the setters, let out the German shepherds. And then the cycle starts all over again.

—Whew! My head's spinning! Alkis tried not to laugh. That seems simple to you? It's like a computer program. Besides, you can never leave.

—Where would I go? I'm only happy when I'm here. Of course I do think about Switzerland every now and then.

Alkis looked at me, laughing.

—Could you keep all those times straight, when to let the dogs in and out?

—I'd mess it up right away, they'd tear each other to shreds.

—Life needs a system, Uncle Miltos said, and turned on the news.

—I'll drop you at your place on my way to Glyfada, Alkis told me.

The whole family saw us out: the lapdogs, the setters, the kids with their ice cream, my cousins, Aunt Louisa and Uncle Miltos.

—See you next Saturday, I told them.

—I'll be coming on Saturdays from now on, too, Alkis said.

In the car we were silent. Alkiviadis didn't take my hand, though he did brush a few dog hairs off my sleeve.

As I opened my door, he said:

—I'll call you.

—But you don't have my number.

—I got it from Louisa. I'll call you, he said again, and smiled.

I stood in the door and watched as his car disappeared around the corner.

35.

Alkiviadis and I saw one another often. Mostly we went
for walks in the country. It was almost winter. Months
had passed since our first encounter at Aunt Louisa's.
We would go on long walks, then sit in a clearing and
talk. We talked for hours, trying to tell each other the
story of our entire lives up until the moment we had
met.

I would listen in wonder as my life unwound itself
before me, with all its difficulty, madness and joy,
acquiring an intense reality through this narration,
while at the same time becoming utterly dreamlike. My
life was confused and chaotic, though beneath the surface, perhaps as with all lives, there was an invisible
structure, a continuity, a hidden purpose. Alkis's life
seemed simpler, but perhaps that was an illusion.
Sprawled out in a clearing, we listened as our lives
unfolded like fairytales. We compared our experiences.
It was as if we were straightening up two messy houses,
getting rid of one piece of furniture to make room for
another. We tried to hold onto the good moments while
banishing the pain and the guilt, the ugliness, the hopelessness. Sometimes I would cry, remembering some
awful event, and Alkis would fold me in his arms.

—You had to get all this out eventually, he would say.
—And there's so much more, I would reply.

—You're getting yourself ready for me. And I'm doing the same, for you.

One day after our walk, Alkis invited me back to his place. When we lay down naked on the bed, Alkis took my face tenderly between his hands.

—Don't be scared, he said. Don't be scared. I would never hurt you. It's not just that I love you. You've become me, you became me, and how could I ever hurt myself?

Later, after Alkis was asleep, I made myself a cup of tea and sat on the edge of the bed. I leaned over and took his hand. In his sleep he squeezed mine, hard. How long did we stay that way? I don't remember. I looked at him. My eyes filled with tears.

This is the man of my life, I thought. I bent and kissed him on the forehead.

36.

Alkis's place became my place, too.

It's night. We switch on the light and smoke silently in one another's arms. Caesar crouches, then pounces on the chairs and sofa, scratching at them with his claws. Alkis laughs.

—I like the scratch marks Caesar leaves on the furniture. Sometimes when he's sleeping, hidden under the bed, I look at them and wonder if he does it on purpose, so I'll think about him even when I can't see him. He's very proud of his claws, and he adores me. He's trying to show me how strong he is, but it's also an act of love.

—Alkis, people are so stingy with their emotions. They want to be loved, but only if it doesn't mess up their lives, their schedules, their clean furniture. How many people do you know who would let their cats scratch up their armchairs?

—Then they live alone with their armchairs. Because the people who love us scratch us, like Caesar. We have to let others be free to show us their love however they choose, however they know, however they can—as long as they don't destroy us. And what is love, anyway? It's clawmarks, scratches, scars, traces someone leaves inside of you. The thing I fear most is stillness, silence. I want permanent marks, life. What's love for you?

part three

—For me, love is white magic.

Caesar awoke, emerged from under the bed, jumped onto Alkis's lap and began kneading his sweater with his paws, purring.

The three of us looked at one another in perfect harmony, like a single being.

37.

These days we were going to Aunt Louisa's together on Saturdays. We had met there, and now we went as a couple. And each time the magic of the estate would wrap itself around us tighter and tighter.

One Saturday Uncle Miltos showed us his enormous collection of photographs of birds from all over the world. He'd pasted them in albums, and beneath each photograph he had written the bird's name in all different languages. The albums just kept coming. We were a little bit bored, but even that boredom was sweet. The hours passed as we listened to the strange, unfamiliar names of eagles, there was a fire in the fireplace, we drank tea, and Alkis held my hand.

Another week we all ate chocolate cake and watched *Gone with the Wind*. Aunt Louisa started crying during the very first scene. It was raining. It was nine p.m., the time when Uncle Miltos always let the German shepherds out of their kennels and locked up the setters. In the movie, during the scene when Rhett Butler gives that legendary kiss to Scarlett next to the river, bending her backward like a reed, Alkis whispered to me:

—Let's go upstairs for a while, alone. I want to talk to you.

We sat down on a small sofa beside the aquariums. The birds were sleeping in their cages.

—I want us to get married, Alkis told me.

I didn't answer.

—I want us to get married.

We were both looking straight ahead, but I could sense Alkis's hands trembling. Time passed. Alkis lit a cigarette, rose, began to pace.

—I'm scared, I said.

—What are you scared of?

—I've never been married before.

—Fortunately, said Alkis, laughing.

—I'm scared.

Just like the first time we made love, months earlier, Alkis took my face in his hands.

—Don't be scared, he told me. Don't be scared. There's nothing to be afraid of with me. And you know it.

I stood up. An uncontrollable rage was blazing up inside me.

—Every time I want to write, I want to write love stories. But as soon as I pick up the pen I'm overcome by horror.

—What does that have to do with us getting married?

—I don't know. But it does. My true nature comes out in my writing. I've only matured in my writing. In real life, I'm at sea.

—Real life? You're talking like a child. There isn't just one life. Haven't you been happy with me for months? Didn't you manage that? Our life is something we create. If you want unhappiness, you'll have it. Happiness is frightening, I agree, and it's much more difficult. You have to break down so many barriers in order to get close to someone. It might seem like a paradox, but unhappiness is easy. Whereas you've got to really love yourself before you can let yourself be happy. You have to believe you deserve it. Otherwise you just can't bear the joy. You'd be happy with me. I know it. Not mindlessly happy, like in fairytales. But you'll start to feel fulfilled—and after that, everything else will fall into place. And you're so ready for it, I just know it. I would never have proposed if you weren't ready. You don't know it yet. But I know.

—Yes, I told him, yes.

—Say the whole thing. I want to hear it.

—Yes. I want to marry you.

In the aquariums, the fish had hidden in their caves. I asked Alkis if fish ever slept. He kissed my hand.

—I'll make you happy, he answered.

38.

The next day I received the first letter from John, from America. That day I was distracted around Alkis. John was a painter. He said flattering things about my book, but really it was a love letter. I wrote back right away. We began an impassioned correspondence. I had no idea what he looked like. We wrote one another letters every day, letters that were thirty pages long. John became a sort of obsession for me. *If he can write so beautifully*, I thought, *he must be beautiful, too.*

He called me his "meteorite," and wrote, *You came to me express in the night as thousands of meteorites fell from the sky. I want to introduce you to the magic of Connecticut.*

In another letter: *Last night you visited me for an hour. You were wearing black, a string of pearls around your neck. For the first time I realized how beautiful you are.*

The letters fell on the house every day, like rain.

Everything is so different with you. You sail through your secret garden and throw me a golden rope with an anchor at the end. I bury the anchor in my garden. Do you like Delvaux? He's so sweet, so tender, and all those sweet, tender women sailing through his paintings look like you. And his men are real men, chiseled from marble, watching the women as they walk, ethereal but real. He has a painting called The

Hands. *The painter's hands are in the work, and there are naked women staring at them. In the background another woman is lying down with a naked boy to make love, but the ground is all rocks, and their hands are in the air, they don't know where to put them. To the left, in the foreground, is a face. It's the painter, Delvaux. He's holding a paintbrush and looking at his work.*

In another letter: *When I paint you, you'll have a string of pearls around your neck, which will flow on your breast like tears, like stars.*
 My house is yellow, fairly large. It's surrounded by a white fence and flowerbeds. Twenty cats play at multiplication in my yard—yesterday they reached fifty.

And another: *I'm sending you a lock of my hair. It lost all its charm as soon as I cut it from my head, but perhaps someday soon you shall caress all of my hair...*
 I'm sending you my white pillow. I swear that I love you.

And another: *Now we are silent, facing one another. Words are no longer necessary. Now that I've spoken to you, I will paint you, paint you for all of eternity. Your hair... your hair... flaming blond like the sun.*
 There among the flowers in my garden, your letter was waiting for me, slightly damp from the morning dew. I opened you and, speechless, put you in my wheelbarrow...

In the happy circus of my life there is a silence. And in that silence your voice is hiding...
   Your meteorite companion.

Woman of water, of the sea, woman of the spring shower, woman with eyes full of tears, Ondine, my muse, my hero, the demon of my art, I adore you for your magic...

Dark ink and sea salt crackled on your little belly...

The clarity of your ambiguous nature... Its power rushes into me with an insane passion...

Distant sleeping child, wash me with your tears, water my garden with your tears, water it each night...

My whole world aches for you to rest your feet upon it. My tears ache to become stars, to flow between your legs. I want to be inside you.

I want to come to America, I wrote back. *But I'm scared of the journey.*
   I'll come and get you, he answered.
   I packed my suitcases, had Lyn vaccinated, and was ready. Ready and fat, though I'd written to John that I was so skinny my cheeks were hollow.

Not to worry, I thought, *love is blind*.

The big day came. John's flight would arrive at eleven, and we would leave together that same evening. I watched the airplanes in the sky. At twelve the doorbell rang. Nervous, I opened the door just a crack, stuck out my hand and grabbed hold of his. He came inside— a skinny, weak blond man who, like me, was trembling.

—Is it you? we said at the same time. We looked at one another.

—I thought you'd be thinner, John told me.

—And I thought you'd be bigger, I answered. We embraced.

—Your bra is bothering me.

—Should I take it off?

—No.

—Did I disappoint you? I asked.

—No. I just thought you'd be thinner.

—And I thought you'd be bigger, I told him. Well, let's open the champagne.

—I don't drink alcohol. Only milk.

I poured some milk into one of the exquisite old champagne glasses. He drank it in a single swallow.

—Would you like more?

—Yes.

He drank an entire bottle of milk. I had prepared caviar and crackers, but they didn't go well with milk, so I hid them.

—Do you have any peanut butter? he asked.

—No, I said, and my eyes welled with tears. Right then I should have said no to it all, but everything was already in motion, there was no going back. I had imagined John as an American intellectual in the body of an enormous basketball player. But he was neither one. He was just American. John and I tried to make love. When he kissed me he slobbered all over me as if he were eating an ice cream. Suddenly he jumped up from the bed.

—I forgot to take my insulin.

I was stunned.

—I'm diabetic. I didn't write about it because I didn't want to disappoint you. I have to give myself shots every few hours, otherwise I'll die. I only eat certain foods: no sweets, just cereal, milk, and bread.

He took his insulin. Lyn, who hates shots, began to bark.

—Let's not make love yet, I told him. Let's get to know one another better.

—Okay, he said, relieved. Then he looked at me. I thought you'd be thinner.

—I don't have diabetes. I eat what I want.

On the plane Lyn was proud, she had her own seat. She was little, so she curled up in her blanket and slept with her plastic bone between her paws. I sat beside her uneasily. I was going to America with a stranger I didn't love, who was diabetic to boot. How much I had loved him when all I had was the letters! Once again my imagination had gotten the better of me. Why couldn't I have fallen in love with some neighbor, the boy next door? No, I had to fall in love via America. And what was I doing now, on a plane with Lyn? The other passengers took their blankets down from the overhead bins. They were speaking all sorts of languages—the plane was a madhouse. They showed us a movie with earphones. I couldn't hear a thing because the man next to me had his headset turned up very loud in Japanese. Then they served us our meal. We began with a pâté.

—It smells funny, John said.

—Seems fine to me. Besides, you can't eat rich foods.

—Don't worry. It's dry, like bread.

John ate the pâté. Before long he was green.

—It was spoiled.

He looked at me with hatred, as if I were to blame.

It occurred to me then that we hadn't exchanged a single tender word since we'd met—and after such passionate letters, such love, such expectation. All we had talked about was food, diabetes and insulin.

John began vomiting nonstop. The movie they were showing was *Tea and Sympathy*. We arrived in New York. It would take another three hours for us to reach Middletown, Connecticut.

—Welcome to New York! John said, and hugged me.

I looked up, saw the skyscrapers, and fainted. I came to in John's truck, sprawled out on my back with Lyn in my arms. I crossed the entire city with my hands over my eyes. Now and then I peeked between my fingers and cried out:

—The buildings are too tall, I can't stand it!

I must have been the only person in the world to ride through New York with my eyes shut.

—Don't look, John said. We're getting close to the Empire State Building.

The next thing I knew, a wild animal was looming above us. I fainted again.

When I came to, we had left New York.

—Are we almost there? I kept asking.

John turned and looked at me. He was furious and pale.

—I told you that pâté was spoiled.

—Is that my fault?

Now we were on a highway. John threw up out the window.

That first day, I had no way of knowing that my arrival in America, with the vomiting and the skyscrapers, would set the tone for my entire stay—two whole months. We drove endlessly. By now John was extremely sick. He kept throwing up out the window, and was white as a sheet.

—John, you're even skinnier than before, I told him.

I thought again of our passionate letters. I kissed him on the cheek.

—John, it'll pass. I'll take care of you when we get there. I still love you, John. You'll see.

John leaned over to throw up out the window.

—We're going to have to stop at a motel. I'm really sick. I can't drive anymore.

All I'd seen of America was New York, sprawled on my back, and highways. Now I'd be introduced to motels, too.

—Could I have a glass? John asked at the reception desk.

—Sorry, the kitchen is closed.

It was nine p.m.

—I have to take some medicine, John insisted. How am I supposed to take it without a glass?

—Sorry, it's closed.

The motel room reminded me of *Lolita*. It was luxurious, but in a cheap, shabby way. John paced the room with a pill in his palm. Suddenly he grabbed an ashtray, washed it well, drank the tiny bit of water the ashtray would hold, and tried to swallow his pill.

—I did it, he said, exhausted, and collapsed onto the bed.

I lay down too.

Our arrival in America will be triumphant, he had written in one of his letters.

I fell asleep. I dreamed that I was going up to the top of the Empire State Building. There was no elevator, only stairs, and it took me days to go all the way up. All the windows were open and the wind rushed in from all sides—it was like climbing a mountain, but a mountain that was also a prison. I had a basket of food with me, and whenever I got tired I would stop to eat and birds would fly in and ask me what time it was. Finally I reached the top. It was very cramped. I looked around and saw that thing they call New York, tall buildings ruining the sky. The buildings were looking at one another and I was looking at them, and I liked it a lot, it was like company. Then the sky darkened, God was angry, and the buildings began to bend to the right with such grace, like trees. They bent and bent and lay down on the sidewalk and closed their windows like eyes, they were tired and went to sleep. Then the Empire State Building asked me to leave so it could sleep, too. And so I left.

We checked out of the motel at five the next morning. John was fine.

—We should be there in two hours, he told me.

We entered the state of Connecticut. Day was breaking. The scenery was breathtakingly beautiful. There were enormous red trees, flowers and squirrels, and the sky seemed bigger than the sky in Europe. During my entire stay, those were the only moments when I felt a sort of euphoria, something that connected me to the place I was visiting. We passed a sign that read "Middletown" and entered a town that reminded me of Hansel and Gretel. Everything was small and doll-like: little wooden houses were nestled in the forest, freckled kids rode by on bicycles. The whole town was lost in space and time, like a dream.

—We're here, John said.

We had stopped in front of a two-story New England–style wooden house with a garden full of roses and vegetables. It's my only beautiful memory of America: the sun lighting up that splendid landscape, inching across the façade of the house, a squirrel peering at me from its perch atop of a head of cabbage. Everything else is clouded in a mist, part of a tragicomic nightmare that could only have happened in that country.

John had decorated the inside of the house. He had written "Welcome" everywhere in gold and silver garlands. I felt sorry for him, and lay down beside him in the bedroom.

—I'll stay here until you fall asleep.

—Yes, he said, yes.

He fell asleep right away. Lyn and I carefully got up and went into the kitchen. Poor John had filled two whole cupboards with dog food, Country Dinner and Yiam-Yiam. Lyn ate two cans. I made myself some coffee and lit a cigarette. I stayed like that until noon, sitting in a chair with Lyn on my lap, not knowing what to do, where to go, what to think.

John woke up.

—You know, he told me, you're much older than I am.

—And fatter, I snapped.

I took Lyn and went to sit in the yard, slamming the door behind me.

And so began our everyday life. John worked at the university. He got up at five to paint, left at eight, and came home every evening at six. So there I was, completely alone with Lyn in a town like the one in *Peyton Place*, where I didn't know a soul. I was in the heart of the country, not in New York, but in middle-class America. Though I didn't realize it at the time, the one benefit of my trip was that in time I got to know the real country, not just the one I'd seen in movies. In the beginning, though, Lyn really saved me. She seemed to sense my despair. She was always sitting on my lap or barking for me to open the door so we could run around in the fields. There in Connecticut I came to adore Lyn. She was my only companion and she tried to keep me entertained, in all the ways her dog's mind could think up.

I decided to clean the whole house. I put on a kerchief and apron and started to mop. As I scrubbed the floors I imagined myself at some literary cocktail party in New York, in a black dress with a high neckline and open back. I'd come here hoping to find myself at the center of intellectual life, eating *petits fours* while chatting about Faulkner, and here I was with a kerchief on my head, sweeping and scrubbing a diabetic's house in Middletown, Connecticut.

One night John asked:

—Why don't you want to?

—I can't, I told him, I can't. From now on I'll sleep on the couch with Lyn.

After that John changed, became hostile. But the poor thing was so puny and weak that even his aggression seemed polite. We never talked anymore. The house was divided in two. I was alone all day, and I was alone in the evenings after John came home. My love for Lyn became insane, almost erotic. "Lyn," I would say, "Lyn." She was a small, golden-haired dog, not too smart, though perhaps that's why I adored her the way I did. And her love for me made her so sensitive that she acquired a sort of intelligence.

part three

Every morning I swept and mopped both floors of the
house. I had been seized by a mania for cleanliness.
Around noon I watched *General Hospital*. Gradually I
sank into lethargy, until I didn't even know where I was.
I was imprisoned in America.

Across the street was a big, beautiful house. I would
often look over and see men in boots and jeans sitting
on the porch, talking or playing cards. They were the
only people I'd seen in Middletown besides the milk-
man. One day I crossed the road.
—Hello, I said.
—Hello there, they replied.
—I'm Greek.
—How nice.
—Is this a hotel?
They burst out laughing.
—Something like that.
I began to go every day, and even taught them new
card games.
—Why do you all live here together? I always asked.
—Why do you live across the street? they'd reply,
winking.
One evening I told John about going to see them
every day. The fork dropped from his hand.
—Are you insane? he cried. Are you completely

insane? Those men are criminals, long-term convicts. They've been released from prison on probation, and if they commit even the smallest offense they'll be locked back up again. Middletown is so small and quiet that they've put even the most dangerous men in that house: murderers, rapists, all of them convicted of the most hideous crimes. Don't ever go there again, do you hear me? They put them on this street because there's nothing else around.

—I know very well there's nothing else around, that's why I go to see them.

John started sobbing

—You've told me you have all these phobias, yet you go over to chat with murderers? Then he whispered, Why did I ever have to read your book?

And thus my social life came to an end.

One morning I woke at five to a rain so hard I thought the dam on the river must have burst. Rain fell around the house like a curtain, in drops as big as eggs. By then my apathy was so extreme that when I saw a house sailing by like a boat, swept off by the flood, I didn't even wake up John. I just whispered to myself, "Look, there's a house going by." Though I did turn on the radio:

—*Connecticut has been hit by the worst flooding in a century. Hundreds are dead, houses have been torn from their foundations. All of Connecticut is one huge sea. Fortunately many of the houses are wooden, and float. But the storm is still raging, especially in Middletown. This tragedy will doubtless claim countless lives, as the rain is expected to continue for quite some time.*

There I was in my nightgown, stepping outside with Lyn in my arms. The water had risen above my knees. For the first time I ran over to our neighbor's house. His name was Hans Brenneman, and he was Jewish. I'd never dared go to his house before.

—Mr. Brenneman, I cried, Mr. Brenneman!

—Oh… my dear neighbor. I was wondering when you would finally come to see me. So it took a Second Coming for us to meet. Come in, dry off by the fire. It's five a.m., and I always watch *Love Boat* in the mornings. How about a bowl of ice cream?

And so, with houses gliding by on all sides, I watched *Love Boat* and ate vanilla ice cream with chocolate syrup. It was my happiest day in America. Mr. Brenneman tucked his coat around my shoulders.

—You know, he said, I've always loved movies like *The Ten Commandments*. I enjoy the spectacle. And here we have it firsthand, and for free.

The houses glided by and disappeared into the darkness created by the rain. On *Love Boat* beautiful girls swam in a pool on the deck of a ship.

—I'm an old man, Mr. Brenneman told me. I'd be

lying if I told you I wasn't enjoying the floods, and at my age lying is a luxury I can't afford. I like anything that takes my mind off my loneliness. Biblical catastrophes fascinate me more and more as I age. Besides, this house is made of cement. I'm old and I'm Jewish. I'm retired. My children—that's them, in the photographs on top of the TV—they've all left. They never write to me. Will you come and see me often?

Each morning at five I was there, watching *Love Boat* with Mr. Brenneman. The whole state of Connecticut had turned into one big river. We would watch *Love Boat* and listen as huge trees uprooted themselves and traveled off, squirrels trapped in their branches. And always there was the drumbeat of rain, the curtain of rain that closed us off so reassuringly from the outside world. Each day I stayed longer and longer. I would run over to Mr. Brenneman's house with Lyn early each morning and sit by the fire to dry my rain-soaked night-gown. I had completely forgotten John. All the love I'd felt for him from afar, before I met him, had now been transferred to Mr. Brenneman.

In the ashes of the fire Mr. Brenneman made a kind of dessert I'd never had before, something called marshmallows, and then we would eat ice cream. We watched TV while outside all of Middletown floated away. After *Love Boat* we watched *All My Children, Trip to Heaven, Celebrity,* and *To Conquer Manhattan.*

—Mr. Brenneman, you remind me of my uncle Harilaos. When I was little, he used to play chess on our marble floor tiles, or on the plaid suits of our guests. Then one day he disappeared. We never saw him again, alive or dead. He didn't take anything with him, not even his passport.

Mr. Brenneman really liked this story. He made me tell it three times.

Those mornings when I ran half-naked with Lyn in my arms through the incessant downpour to Mr. Brenneman's, those endless hours in front of the TV, with the ice cream and the marshmallows, came to seem more and more like a dream. Mr. Brenneman would tell me about his life. It had been a hard life, full of pain, hardship, and disappointment, but he talked about it with such humor that we laughed constantly, as if he were telling jokes. Our friendship turned into adoration. One day I had a cold and didn't go until the following morning.

—I couldn't sleep at all last night, he told me.

We hugged, then sat down to watch our shows.

Mr. Brenneman had a wisdom that stemmed from his Jewish roots. One day he said:

—The people we truly love either leave or die.

And another morning:

—Love that dog as much as she loves you. I see her eyes when she looks at you; those are human eyes.

And another time:

—When I die, I want to go to the paradise of the Jews. I love you very much. In you, God has granted me one last child.

It was Mr. Brenneman who really saved me in America. Perhaps the whole purpose of my trip was to bring us together. He laughed when I said that in a country where everyone jogged and ate cereal, he was the only one who drank coffee and smoked cigars.

—Love, he told me. Love everything from the grass to the first person who walks by in the street. Love it all. That's the only thing that can make life not just bearable, but beautiful. Me… I've loved a lot in my day.

The days passed, more and more dreamlike. By now I went to John's house only to sleep.

The day came when I was to return home. I went over to Mr. Brenneman's with Lyn and my suitcase. He was standing at the front door in his suit.

—The trip was worth it, I told him.

—I'll miss you, he answered. My last child is leaving.

We corresponded for years. I never really got to know America, but America introduced me to Mr. Brenneman. One day my letter came back unopened. Mr. Brenneman had died. And with his death, America vanished altogether from my mind, as if I had never gone.

When I got home, I accepted Alkis's proposal of marriage. He was furious.

—But as soon as I proposed, you went all the way across the Atlantic!

—Do you want to get married or not? I asked him.

—I do. His eyes filled with tears. I'll suffer a lot with you, he added.

—Yes, I said. A lot.

39.

Vanessa was British. And a lesbian. I met her at a party thrown by a British veterinarian, a colleague of Alkis's. She was very tall and so fat that when I first saw her, I thought an enormous tree had uprooted itself and was marching toward me, like in *Macbeth* when the whole forest charges the castle.

That evening I was wearing a black dress with a high neckline and a back that was open almost to the waist.

—That's a beautiful dress.

I heard a deep voice behind me and thought it was a man. Turning around, I saw a gigantic woman studying me through a gold monocle.

—My name is Vanessa Prévoit.

—I'm Alkis's wife.

—I know. I asked about you. I was struck by the way you smoke so many different brands of cigarettes. All night I've been watching as you smoke brand after brand. It even occurred to me that your handbag might have a false bottom. That's a Dunhill, if I'm not mistaken.

—Yes, that's right. They're my favorite. I smoke all the other brands around the Dunhills, if you know what I mean. When I finally have the incredible pleasure of lighting one by chance, just from rummaging around in my bag, I know it's a Dunhill right away, from the taste and smell. Usually at events like this I hide in the bathroom and smoke it alone, in peace.

—Wonderful! Wonderful! said Vanessa, rubbing her hands together. I think the two of us will be great friends. I, too, am... how shall I say? A little *excentrique*... in dress, and in other things, too.

I looked at her. She was wearing a huge black velvet hat with a feather and a ruby brooch in the shape of a tiger. The eyes of the tiger were two glittering green emeralds.

—Your eyes look like the eyes of the tiger on my hat, said Vanessa.

—I like your brooch, I replied.

—So do I. I bought it in Venice one Christmas, to cheer myself up.

—You must have been very sad, to buy such an expensive brooch.

—Yes, I was. It's been years now, but in Venice, I was left by someone I adored. We parted ways in the Piazza San Marco, in the rain. To console myself, I went to Rome and shopped all day, crying the whole time.

—You loved him that much?

Vanessa's smile was enigmatic.

—Yes, she answered.

A few months later, after we had started spending a lot of time together, Vanessa told me that the man who had left her in Venice was really a woman. Her name was Esmeralda.

The night I met her, Vanessa was wearing a long black cashmere dress with billowing sleeves. She was always gesturing with her hands, so her sleeves kept hitting me in the face as we spoke. She looked like a gigantic black butterfly, and her hat with its feather reminded me of Porthos from *The Three Musketeers*. She was wearing lots of expensive jewelry. But the jewels seemed to lose something of their shine on her, because there was nothing the least bit feminine about Vanessa.

As we left the reception she leaned over and whispered in my ear:

—My dress is by Kenzo.

I'll never forget how Vanessa looked the night I met her. With her black hat and her short, curly red hair, her huge dress, her tortoise-shell cigarette holder and gold monocle, she made all the other women at the reception seem badly dressed and ordinary.

We began spending a lot of time together. At first Alkis

wasn't jealous, since the two of us would make fun of Vanessa behind her back, and besides, he knew I wasn't attracted to women.

But the first time he asked me, "Isn't Vanessa extraordinarily ugly?" I knew he'd begun to be jealous.

Perhaps it was because I had started to avoid talking about her. I no longer told him where we went, as I had when I'd first become friends with her. And then a friend of Alkis's told him how he'd seen us dancing at a disco, barefoot and crazed.

By now I saw Vanessa every day. She would pick me up in her black Jaguar and we'd drive for hours, listening to music. In the evenings she would take me to expensive restaurants, and then we usually ended up in some disco where we would dance until dawn.

Vanessa always walked in front and I followed behind. It made me feel as if there were an enormous umbrella sheltering me. Whenever we went out to eat Vanessa would sail into the restaurant like a frigate, and I would scamper in after her, microscopically small. We'd sit down at a table. I would toss our packs of cigarettes onto the tablecloth. We would drink, smoke, eat, and above all talk, sometimes until morning.

What drew me to Vanessa was her exuberance, which was as oversized as her dresses. Actually, everything about her was huge. Her purse looked like a suitcase. Her clothes flapped in the streets, brushing against passersby. Her enormous hats split the air like the sails of a ship.

She always wore tennis shoes with her expensive dresses, but handmade ones, custom designed for her. She had a pair dyed to match every dress she owned; she must have had a hundred pair.

She was also extremely generous. She would leave tips bigger than our bills. And she bought me expensive gifts almost every day—clothes, furs, jewelry, or sometimes just a cheap barrette. "This'll look beautiful in your blond hair," she'd say. But when she gave me a TV and a VCR she had ordered from London especially for me, the latest designs on the market—then, for the first time, Alkis got angry.

—I have no intention of watching TV and movies on gifts from Vanessa.

Suddenly he raised his voice, which he did only rarely.

—Enough! he said. I've had it! If you like Vanessa so much, why don't you go and live with her? You know, I haven't seen you in a month. At night when I come home from the office, I'm tired and hungry. The house is a mess, with presents from Vanessa scattered every-where—yesterday I found a fur in my study. And the fridge is always empty, so every night I go out and eat junk food. I've gained ten kilos from all the pizza and sausage pies. And so far I've put up with it all. But to watch the news on Vanessa's TV—that's going too far!

—Fine, Alkis, I told him. Don't you see that Vanessa is just my friend, that you're jealous of her the same way you're jealous of anyone who gets too close to me? Fine, Alkis, I'll go and stay with her. Besides, I need a vacation, a vacation from you.

That night as I packed my bags Alkis sat beside me, smoking a cigarillo. There were tears in his eyes.

—Don't go, he begged me. Don't leave me again, darling. You can see Vanessa as much as you like, it doesn't bother me, I like her, too. And I know that, deep down, you're as pure and innocent as a dove. My lovely little dove, please don't leave. Whatever you want you can have here, too, with me, we can share it. You're always leaving. Please stop leaving, it kills me every time.

I didn't answer. I carried my bags to the door and called for a taxi.

It was Christmas. I'd been living with Vanessa since September. We had decided to spend New Year's in Italy.

—It's the most beautiful season, she told me. Have you ever seen Venice in the cold and rain? After that

we'll go to Perugia, to Assisi, where St. Francis was
born, and we'll end up in Rome.

Vanessa bought me new Vuitton suitcases. They
were lined with brown silk printed with tiny black flowers. She also bought all sorts of creams to protect my
face from the cold. I liked one of them in particular,
because of its name: Dramatically Different Moisturizing Lotion.

Our flight was to leave the next morning at six. That
night, as I was drifting off to sleep, I thought of Alkis.
For a moment I missed him, yearned for him. Then I
fell asleep.

First stop: Venice. It was freezing, six degrees below
zero. And it wasn't raining, as Vanessa had promised.
The moisture from the sea seeped into my bones, making me dizzy. We checked into a luxury hotel, the
Danieli, Vanessa sweeping in first, I scampering in after
her.

A man at the reception desk took our passports.

—*Si, si, Signora Prévoit*, he said. *La camera matrimoniale… Si, si. Va bene, Signora Prévoit.*

He turned to me and winked. I felt strangely
embarrassed, without knowing why.

—*Bella donna*, the man said to Vanessa, looking at me. *Molto bella...* Then he smiled. *É una bambola*, he added, looking now at Vanessa.

The hotel was next to the La Fenice opera house, where *La Traviata* was playing.

Our room had a fridge full of soda and pink champagne. A big basket of exotic fruit sat on the table.

There was only one bed.

—But I asked for a room of my own, I said to Vanessa.

—There weren't any, she answered hurriedly, staring at her shoes. And the bed is so big, you won't even know I'm there.

Vanessa looked at me.

—Does it bother you so much to sleep in the same bed as me?

I spent the whole night in an armchair. I couldn't sleep, I was plagued by a persistent worry: did Antonio, the man at the reception desk, think I was a lesbian, too? The thought bothered me so much that by six in the morning I couldn't stand it anymore. I got dressed and went down to the lobby. Antonio was behind the desk, snoring.

The walls and floor of the lobby were swathed in red velvet. There were potted palms and yucca plants in the corners, and little ivory tables.

Antonio woke up. I didn't know a word of Italian, and he didn't speak anything else.

—Antonio, I said, *mio marito* is waiting for me at home, he knows I'm traveling with Vanessa. I'll be calling him in a little while, he's expecting me to call at eight.

Antonio smiled and lit a cigarette.

—Signorina, why are you telling me this? It's none of my business. Besides...

He broke into laughter.

—*Io, signora, sono un...* gay! *Capisci? Io amo Angelo. Ma, Angelo cattivo, cattivo!*

Antonio took a deep drag from his cigarette, stubbed it out and immediately lit another. He was on the verge of tears.

—*Io, non* gay, *Antonio, capisci?* I said. *Io, amo...*

I'd forgotten the Italian word for what I wanted to say.

—*Io, amo...* Men!

—*Si, signora... Si...* To gay or not to gay... *Che importanza? Il sex é uno oggetto misterioso... Signora Vanessa é molto generosa... É molto chic... Vuole un cafe espresso?*

We drank our coffee and watched the sun lighting up the *palazzi*.

—*Venezia...* Antonio said. *É molto bella...*

—*Si...* I answered.

—*Cattivo Angelo... Cattivo...* Antonio kept whispering.

I went back up to our *camera matrimoniale*.

—Where were you? Vanessa asked.

—Down with Antonio, at the reception desk. We drank an espresso.

For the first time, my tone of voice was hostile.

—Don't talk to strangers, she told me. We have a lot of money with us, and Italians are shameless thieves. What did you and Antonio talk about, anyway?

—He told me he was gay.

I looked Vanessa straight in the eye.

—And he's convinced I'm a lesbian.

—Does that bother you? Vanessa asked.

—Yes!

—And why did he think that?

—Because I'm with you.

We left the hotel that morning at ten. The temperature was the usual six below, but now a strong wind had come up, too, making the cold almost unbearable.

Vanessa was wearing a black velvet cape, a green hat and high green boots. She hit a passerby with her cape, nearly knocking him to the ground. I was wearing tennis shoes and before long I was freezing. My feet were completely soaked. I took off my socks and wrung them out into the Grand Canal.

Vanessa put on her monocle and opened the guide book.

—Today we'll go to the Gallerie dell'Accademia. It's got an exquisite painting by Giorgione.

Vanessa started walking and I followed her, shivering. We climbed into a *motoscafo*. A fat Italian woman gave us a vicious look, then whispered something to her friend. They laughed. I tucked my scarf over my chest. I was cold.

At the museum Vanessa started telling me when each painter had been born, reading so loudly from her book that a crowd gathered around us, thinking she was the museum guide. The real guide, an Italian with white hair and a moustache, had gone off to complain to the guards.

I stopped short before a painting: Giorgione's *La Tempesta*.

I felt my breath stop and my legs start to tremble. I stared at the painting. Everything around me disappeared.

In a mysterious landscape, a thunderstorm is about to break. A woman, naked from the waist down and with one breast exposed, is holding a baby in her arms as if about to nurse it. Opposite her, at the other edge of the painting, against a background of foliage, a man in breeches and a red waistcoat stands watching her. She's looking off, somewhere else. The man is carrying a staff. There is a sweet sense of anticipation—perhaps of approaching rain. There is a silence, a calm. The two figures have finally arrived at their destination, after ages of wandering and pain.

The landscape is shady, full of green trees and white clouds with curves as round as a woman's breasts.

Water gushes from a spring. Or perhaps it's a river.

I closed my eyes.

I forgot all about Vanessa, and Venice, and Alkis.

A sweet euphoria washed over me, though something like a premonition sat heavy on my chest.

I pictured myself in a similar landscape. But I was alone: the man in the painting had disappeared.

I was lying in the shade of a large green tree. A spring gushed beside me.

I put my hand into the crystalline water.

In this complete silence, I fell asleep.

Much later, I seemed to wake from a dream.

I heard Vanessa's voice coming from far away, like an echo.

—Here, you see, in this painting, the woman

doesn't want the man to see her naked, that's why she's hiding her breast with the baby's head. She despises him. And he's looking at her so hopelessly because he knows she'll never be his. The low clouds, the storm that's about to break, all signal some approaching catastrophe. That's why the painting is called *La Tempesta*.

Vanessa drew close to me, practically gluing her chest to my back, then bent and whispered in my ear:

—Deep down, women don't really want men, they just don't know it. Men saddle women with children, and women don't want children. They want to be free, but they don't dare even consider it. Men always make them suffer. In pregnancy, in childbirth—and then once the babies are born the men no longer desire the women. They lock them up in the house with all those howling babies, the pacifiers and the loneliness.

And the women paint their nails red again and again, watching soaps on daytime TV, while inside them stirs this need to escape, to escape from the man.

Meanwhile, the man goes out every morning to interact with the people around him. He constructs the world, changing it to suit his needs and desires.

And in the evening when he comes home, dinner is ready and warm on the table, the babies are sleeping and his wife is freshly showered. She's even dabbed perfume behind her ears and on her wrists, since those are the first places he'll kiss that night in bed.

But as time passes, she paints her nails deeper and deeper shades of red, and stops watching her shows on TV. She leaves the house and walks through the city, enjoying the way other men look at her, strangers. Later, she goes out only for herself—the gazes of men no longer interest her.

She paints her nails, washes her hair every day, wanders through the city, smokes in the streets, goes window-shopping, maybe ducks into a bookstore to buy a book she'll never read, just for the pleasure of seeing it wrapped up in a package. She sits down at some café, and now, finally, she's the one who looks at the men. And when she starts looking at men she is finally free and invulnerable, because she's finally obtained a gaze, her own gaze, the one her husband stole from her when he locked her up in the house, hiding the outside world from her, the cities and streets, the shops, the other gazes.

By now Vanessa was stroking my neck.

—And once the woman is free from the man, she continued, she seeks out some other woman. Because only another woman can understand her, only a woman will let her be free to travel with her body and her mind, will open up the world to her, instead of hiding it the way a man would. Only a woman will let her finally be a woman, and not just the object of masculine desires.

The two women mirror one another; there's no war anymore, no antagonism.

And these new women will overturn the world, because bit by bit they're stealing the man's world and building it all over again from the beginning, according to their own needs and desires.

And in sex, only a woman can completely satisfy another woman, because they're the same.

Do you want it? Vanessa asked. Do you? Tell me that you do.

I looked at the painting, then at Vanessa. My eyes were so filled with hatred that she took a step back, as if I'd hit her.

—Vanessa, I *have* freed myself from men. That's why I came with you on this trip.

But I freed myself in order to be alone, not with another woman. For me freedom means solitude, a solitude full of walks in the country, solitary strolls through unfamiliar cities, books scattered around my bed at night, lying open at random pages.

And I paint my nails a dark red, but I paint them for myself.

When I'm sitting at a café, I look at my hand resting on the table, my pale hand with its long red nails, maybe I'm wearing a ring, and it fills me with an indescribable pleasure, because that hand is my hand, and I've made it beautiful for myself, and when I leave this café in this unfamiliar city, I'll return to the hotel, take a hot, fragrant bath, and then fall asleep. My solitude is sacred. I won't let anyone take it from me anymore—not Alkis, not you.

I want to be alone, to sail like a ship and stop at whatever harbor I choose, and leave again when I want.

Everything else is the real solitude: to be tied down, to a man or a woman. Let's not kid ourselves—you'd lock me up in a prison, just like Alkis. Maybe even worse.

On the way out I bought a postcard of *La Tempesta*. I sent it to Alkis, with a note on the back: *Only you would understand the beauty and mystery of this painting. I'm starting to get tired of Vanessa, and Venice. It's very cold. Kisses.*

That night we went to Harry's Bar. Vanessa ordered a bottle of pink champagne.

—Drink, she kept telling me, filling my glass again and again.

By three in the morning, I was completely drunk. I climbed up onto a table and sang from *La Traviata*. Everyone in the bar clapped.

Antonio winked at me from behind the reception desk.
    Back in the room, I collapsed onto the double bed. Vanessa lay down beside me. I fell asleep in her arms.

We left the hotel early the next morning. We walked endlessly through the narrow alleyways around the Basilica di San Marco. The temperature had reached seven below. Vanessa was wearing a Black Glamour fur, a huge wool scarf, and sunglasses. I was wearing a fur hat of Alkis's that was too big for me and kept falling down over my eyes. I could hardly see a thing, and I looked like a Russian peasant.
    Vanessa walked quickly a few paces ahead. All I could see from beneath my wide fur hat was her boots hitting the cobblestones rhythmically.

Our relationship had changed since the previous evening. Vanessa kept putting her arm around my shoulder or stroking my cheek, and sometimes she even stopped and waited for me to catch up, something she'd never done before.

Through all of this I remained silent. And when I did talk to her, there was a hostile edge to my voice. I complained constantly of the cold, as if Vanessa were to blame for the weather.

—Venice is nicer in summer, I told her. I even like the tourists. That romantic myth about Venice in winter, that it's more beautiful or more mysterious, is nonsense. Just because Byron and Chopin liked Venice in winter, does that mean I have to like it, too? Besides, they were lunatics. Byron came to celebrate Christmas in Venice with a whole train to himself, and a wagon with lions and tigers following behind. Chopin came to Venice in winter to die. At least he died in the arms of George Sand—I like her, she smoked cigars and wrote novels. But the two of us, Vanessa, really, what are we doing here? We're not crazy, and we're not writers. Couldn't we have come in summer like everybody else?

I burst into tears.

—You're delirious, Vanessa told me, you're delirious from the cold. Let's go have some tea at the Café Royal so you can pull yourself together. Besides, I told a friend of mine, the writer Ilona Pearl, that I would meet her there. She and her girlfriend live in Venice now, in Giorgio Caputo's *palazzo*. I haven't seen her in years. Blow your nose, get a hold of yourself. I don't want Ilona to see you like this.

—Piazza San Marco is so festive in summer, with the orchestras playing different songs all at the same time, I went on, still crying. Now the two of us wander through a deserted Venice, and the stairs of the *palazzi* leading down to the water look like they're sinking into a frozen green muck. It scares me. Why don't we leave today for Perugia?

—Whatever you want, Vanessa answered icily. After all, this trip is for you. If you're disappointed with Venice in winter it's because you don't see the beauty in this abandoned city, with its low sky, the piercing cold and the emptiness. But I forgot, she added sarcastically, you're a child of the sun, you sit on the beach and bake for hours on end.

It was as if she'd uttered the worst of all insults.

—You're disappointed, too, I answered.

—By what?

I looked at her, but didn't say a thing. Vanessa nervously took off her hat. Her red hair glowed beneath the black, steely sky.

Vanessa's friend Ilona was waiting for us at the Café Royal. She introduced us to her girlfriend, Lazy. The four of us drank our tea in silence, watching the rain hit the windowpanes.

Ilona reminded me of Virginia Woolf a few hours

before her suicide. Her friend Lazy looked like a weasel. Ilona didn't talk at all, just gazed out at the rain, or at Lazy. Lazy looked at me, and I looked at my rain-soaked shoes.

We walked for hours through the narrow streets, all four of us silent, always moving. That endless labyrinth of alleyways seemed like a nightmare. The shops were all closed, and the rain had become torrential. There was an amusement park close to our hotel and the opera house. With the gold of the *palazzi* and the frozen beauty of the landscape as a background, the park, with its booths and little pink lights, looked hideous, like an abandoned stage set ready for the trash. I asked Vanessa if we could walk in some other direction, or all go into the hotel.

—No, she told me. We're going to see everything.

That sentence revealed to me how miserly Vanessa really was. She didn't want to miss anything, she wanted to see it all, to consume it. Even her extravagant spending, I realized, always had an ulterior motive. Now that motive was me.

At the amusement park the four of us played various games, always in silence. Rain filled the glasses at the shooting range; Lazy's black hair dripped and shone;

Vanessa's green hat filled up like a little lake. I won a gigantic, fluffy pink bear with a red bow around its neck. It was utterly soaked, so heavy with rain that I could barely pick it up.

—What am I going do with it? I asked in despair. The three women looked at me wordlessly. I started to cry.

—Give it to Alkis when you get home, Vanessa said, in such a spiteful and bitter tone that I suddenly felt sorry for her.

—Don't cry, Ilona said. It's not you, it's Venice. Everyone cries here in winter, every day.

She put her arm around Lazy's waist and they left without saying goodbye.

I picked up the bear and, for the first time, walked ahead, leaving Vanessa to follow behind.

Back at the hotel I gave the bear to Antonio.

—*Per Angelo*, I told him.

—*Oh! Grazie, signora! Grazie! Angelo é un bambolo. Oh! Che bella!*

Antonio kissed me on the cheek.

Vanessa walked right by us. She crossed the lobby with her sleeves billowing. On her way she knocked a Ming vase of red roses to the floor. She looked furious.

part three

Antonio whispered to me:
—*Signora Vanessa… é cattiva?*

That night we went to the casino.

The porter was wearing a red velvet uniform with gold buttons. Vanessa had on a loose dress of purple silk with green and yellow butterflies on its sleeves. I was wearing an evening gown.

Vanessa went into the casino first, hitting the porter in the face with her sleeve. She put a cigarette in her tortoiseshell holder, asked him for a light, and gave him an enormous tip, all so astonishingly fast that the porter was overwhelmed and, in his confusion, looked at Vanessa and stammered:

—*Grazie*, sir!

The casino was in a Venetian *palazzo.* The high ceilings were painted with gold cherubs and white clouds.

The ladies, *en grande toilette*, were mostly elderly and heavily made up. They had handsome young escorts to light their cigarettes and bring them drinks. The young men were all wearing tuxedos and Cartier watches. The croupiers' voices came drifting out of the various rooms in which the ladies were placing their chips on the green felt, choosing their numbers carefully.

121

I'd never been to a casino before. Soon I was drunk on the players' single-minded concentration. The outside world vanished. The casino was like a cruise ship, and we were willing prisoners in a luxury-class cell. The women's perfumes intermingled, and the din of conversation, though deafening, was oddly like silence, hypnotizing you, since all you heard was the croupiers' voices, and the ladies calling out numbers:

—I'll take seven.

—The same, again.

—Twenty-two.

—Put my chips on three again.

The ladies were seated at the roulette tables, their escorts standing behind them. Forgotten cigarettes burned themselves out in the ashtrays. Gold lighters and long cigarette holders just like Vanessa's lay on the green felt. Some of the women had taken off their rings so they would be more comfortable while they played. The green felt sparkled with sapphires, rubies, and diamonds, the glitter of precious stones echoing the glitter of the chandeliers. It reminded me of an operating room when the lights come on and in the absolute silence you hear the surgeon's instructions, the metallic clang of surgical instruments being picked up or set down on the table.

—Now we'll play, too, Vanessa announced. Take

these, and follow your instincts.

The sum was enormous. As soon as I took the chips I forgot all about Venice and Alkis; I even forgot myself. My eyes shone, like those of the other players. My cheeks burned and I shivered as if I were feverish.

As if in a dream, I watched Vanessa play and lose, bid again on the same number, and lose again.

Huge sums now found their way onto the table. Like a voracious animal, the roulette wheel devoured houses, jewels, entire estates. It was three in the morning, and the stakes had gotten high.

The women's makeup was melting on their faces; deep wrinkles began to show like scars on their cheeks and around their eyes. Red nails as sharp as scalpels placed the chips on the felt, arranging them in combinations, or putting them all on one number, the same number again and again.

Vanessa kept losing. She was bathed in sweat and her silk dress stuck to her body, revealing her enormous belly. She was wearing her monocle and kept running her right hand through her frizzy hair, which, drenched with sweat, bristled out from her head like wire.

Only the croupier remained impeccable, without a single wrinkle in his uniform, as he repeated the same phrases in a remote, indifferent voice, like a liturgy:

—*Faites vos jeux.*
—*Oui, Madame, je mise pour vous sur le huit.*
—*Je place sur le neuf, quinze et seize.*
—*Faites vos jeux.*

I put all my chips on number nine.
—Are you out of your mind? Vanessa hissed. If you lose, you'll lose everything. Play a combination.
—You've been losing all night, I retorted. And now you're giving me advice? Didn't you tell me to follow my instincts?
The croupier took my chips and placed them deftly on the green felt. There were so many that he had to stack them in three piles. The number nine disappeared beneath my chips.

A deep silence fell around the table. No one in the casino had ever bet such an amount, and certainly not on a single number. For that round, no one else played. The table was all mine. The croupier's eyes met mine; his gaze held a question, and I nodded almost imperceptibly.
—*Les jeux sont faits*, he said.
He tossed the ball onto the wheel and gave it a solid spin. The wheel began to move more and more slowly, the ball pausing for a moment on one number, then fly-

ing out again, bouncing from number to number with increasing reluctance.

—*Rien ne va plus.*

The wheel made two more full revolutions, then came to a stop.

The ball was on number nine.

The crowd around the table rose and began to clap. Two of Vanessa's friends, Pascale Orage and Marina Del Rey, kissed me on the cheek. I heard someone say:

—*Mais, c'est une fortune!*

I saw Vanessa staring at the ball, pale. I thought I would faint.

Later, at the cashier's, they gave me a paper bag for the money, since it didn't fit in my purse. Again, I walked in front, and Vanessa hurried after me. I left the casino and stepped into a *motoscafo.*

—Piazza San Marco, I said.

At the Danieli I bought a ticket for the train to Rome. Vanessa was crying.

—You're leaving me, just like Esmeralda. Winter in Venice.

She sat on the edge of the bed and lit a cigarette.

—I love you, she said.

—These are yours, I answered.

I threw all the gifts she'd given me onto the bed: the dresses, the jewels, the Vuitton suitcases. I put on my old jeans and t-shirt, and then—taking only my purse, my passport, and the paper bag full of money— I opened the door and left.

I shopped shamelessly in Rome. But this time I bought things I liked. I didn't take my purse with me to the stores. All I took was the money from the casino, which was still in the paper bag they had given me. When I paid, I would take all the money out of the bag, lay it down on the counter, count out whatever I needed, then put the rest away and leave, loaded down with packages.

I stayed at a *pensione* called Casa Frollo that was marvelous, and very cheap. I got up every morning and shopped all day, and at night I would eat alone at the pizzeria next door to the *pensione*.

I spent fifteen days in Rome. The owner of Casa Frollo, Signora Lucia, called me *bambola*. She was very fat, and in the morning she would bring the most wonderful espresso I'd ever had up to my room, while I was still in bed. On my last day there, I went and bought her a silk dress from Yves Saint Laurent that was large and loose and looked just like the dress Vanessa had worn to the casino.

—*Oh! Signora! Che bello! Che bello!*

Signora Lucia went to try it on right away. She looked almost exactly like Vanessa, in those same wide sleeves, the same design—perhaps it really was the exact same dress.

I had bought an enormous set of beige pigskin suitcases, smooth as a pair of gloves. At the airport I had to pay a big fee for exceeding the weight limit.

I drank two bottles of pink champagne on the plane and arrived home in Glyfada blind drunk. The taxi driver shouted and cursed as he unloaded the suitcases from the trunk. Alkis watched dumbfounded as I scrambled up into a tree, singing from *La Traviata*. It was six in the morning. The neighbors came out onto their balconies and started shouting at me to quiet down. Only one old man started singing along.

—Let's go for a swim! Let's all go for a swim! I cried from the tree.

Alkis pulled me down by the feet. I fell into his arms and he carried me into the house, closing the door behind him. He was trembling all over.

—My suitcases! My suitcases! They'll be stolen! I cried.

Alkis carried in every last one of the suitcases, trembling all the while, ghostly pale.

—What's this? What is all this! he shouted, shaking me by the shoulders. What is it? he kept asking, looking down at the countless suitcases, which lined the hall from the front door all the way to the bedroom.

—Gifts from Vanessa! I shouted.

—So she did it, she won you over. Did you make love?

—Constantly, everywhere, we couldn't stop. After each time, she bought me a present. And you can see for yourself, I said, bursting into laughter, there are lots of presents.

Alkis knelt down in front of the suitcases, crying.

—Did you like it? he asked through his sobs.

—I loved it. A woman knows another woman's body better than any man ever can, or at least that's what Vanessa told me when we were at the Gallerie dell'Accademia, looking at Giorgione's *La Tempesta*. We went to Venice, to Assisi in Perugia, where St. Francis was born, and then to Rome. We saw museums, squares, churches, the Vatican. The only thing we didn't do was go to the casino in Venice. Vanessa tried to get me to go, but I wasn't in the mood.

Alkis, on his knees, wrapped his arm around my waist and pressed his cheek against my belly.

 —Stay with me, he said. Don't ever leave again.

40.

I knew right away, the instant I conceived. It was three in the morning on the nineteenth of July. Afterward, Alkis rolled over onto his stomach and whispered:
—I want a child so badly.
Then he fell asleep.
I lit a cigarette and went out onto the terrace.
There was a full moon.

By August nineteenth I still hadn't gotten my period. Glyfada steamed in the heat wave. On the thirtieth, Alkis would be going to England for a veterinarians' conference. I would meet him there in September. The morning he left, as he stood in the door with his suitcases, I told him the results of the test: I was pregnant. He dropped to his knees before me and pressed his cheek against my belly. Then I watched as his car disappeared around the corner.

The heat wave made the landscape barren, like the moon, as the temperature climbed into the forties. The sky turned completely white, viscous. The government was taking emergency measures because of the heat. I stayed alone in the house with Caesar and Lyn. The sea stretching before me was viscous, too, like oil, utterly still, and it had turned a deep green. All day long I sat naked in the sun, smoking. I never left the house. I stared at the sea, lighting one cigarette with the butt of the one before. The house filled with music: *How deep is your love…*, *Just like a woman…*, *Baby, please come back…* I carried the speakers out onto the terrace. The deafening metallic voices poured out into the heat and plunged into the sea. I could feel the baby coursing through my body, from my head to the soles of my feet. I no longer saw anyone at all. I was completely alone with Caesar and Lyn. At night I took Lyn on long walks through the empty city. The darkness was absolute. It was so hot that everyone kept their lights off. Only the TVs were on, glowing like aquariums. As we walked I would hear the sound of the twelve o'clock news drifting out. When we got home Lyn would flop down on the marble floor next to my bed, crossing her front legs and stretching her hind legs behind her, trying to keep cool.

The dreams would begin as soon as I fell asleep. I hadn't dreamed in years. But now I dreamed of the baby. It was angry at me and I didn't know why. It was trying to tell me something. It would make a sharp gesture with the thumb of its right hand: *no*.

—I don't want you! I would shout in my sleep.

—Whether you want me or not, I'm here now, and I'm all settled in. Then it would laugh, a little sadly. Of course it's a little cramped in here, and the heat makes me sweat.

The dreams were always exactly the same, the same words, coming in the same order in the course of each night.

Late at night, I always dreamed that the baby was hanging in my womb like a gigantic centipede, grasping on with its thousands of legs, about to slip out onto the sheets. Its little eyes were full of fear as it slipped further and further down, and tears flowed down its cheeks. Then I would wake with a start, bathed in sweat, my nightgown drenched, sticking to my body.

Whenever I woke in the middle of the night I would remember Alkis, the morning he left for England.

—Be careful, darling, he had said. For our baby's sake. Make sure you walk for two hours every day, and go swimming, and don't smoke. I want this baby more than I've ever wanted anything in my life. I dream of it every night, laughing in your womb, happy because you love it. It's always the same dream: your baby smiles and waves to you with its little hand as if it were far away. "I'm coming!" it cries, "I'm coming! Wait for me!" And you smile back and say, "I can't wait for you to get here!" Darling, I'm so happy! It's part of you, part of the woman I adore, your blood, your flesh. I hope it has my eyes and your hair—I'm insanely happy!

On the morning Alkis left I went out and bought

five cartons of Dunhill Reds. All day I sat in the sun and smoked.

How deep is your love... The music and the heat would rush over me. I would slather tanning oil on my body and hair and lie like that until night fell. Then I would take Lyn for her walk, and then I would go to bed. I did each of these things every day, at exactly the same times. During all of August I didn't go for a single swim.

I felt deeply happy that Alkis was away. Every day we talked on the phone from four to five in the afternoon.

—Are you going swimming? Alkis's voice sounded distant on the telephone. England seemed like another planet.

—Yes, I answered.

—I want this baby.

Every day he told me that on the phone.

—I want it like nothing else in the world.

I stopped going to the gynecologist.

At the beginning of September, during one of his phone calls, Alkis said:

—Let's go to Ireland after the conference and stay there for the rest the month. As a second honeymoon. It'll be good for the baby. I'm so in love with you both.

—Alkis, I've decided not to come. A trip right now might be a strain on the baby, and I don't want anything to upset my pregnancy. Besides, I have a schedule here that I'd rather not upset: an hour of swimming in the morning, a two-hour siesta in the afternoon, a two-hour walk with Lyn in the evening. I'm always in bed by nine. I'm doing everything I can to be a good mother, and that's all I want to concentrate on, even now, before the baby is born.

—Whatever you want, Alkis answered, laughing. Whatever you want, darling. I know how obsessive you are about your schedules. I'll be home at the end of September. We'll go to Ireland next year, with the baby. It'll be a year old. We'll show it the North Sea, how it merges with the green of the mountains at the horizon. At night we'll take it with us to pubs, give it a little beer. I'm so happy! You're going to be such a wonderful mother.

—I'm happy too. This baby means everything to me.

That night I dreamed that I vomited the baby. Like a miscarriage, except it came out my mouth. My mouth flooded with blood and pieces of flesh, tender, sweet-smelling flesh, and I thought I would choke. The baby's hands fastened themselves around my neck, and it screamed: "No, mom, no! Don't do it! I want to live!"

In my dream, I grabbed the two hands that were clutching my neck and pulled with all my strength. I managed to get them off. They were tiny little hands, white and plump, and despite the blood that was choking me, they seemed to smell of jasmine.

Am I crazy? I want this baby, I suddenly thought. But it was already too late. The room had filled with the scent of jasmine from the baby's hands. I woke up with a start, bathed in sweat.

On September nineteenth I was two months pregnant. That evening, on my nightly walk with Lyn, I passed through all the parks in Glyfada, looking at the toddlers. They were playing on seesaws and swings, or with pails in the sand, running and chittering like birds. They plunged their little hands deep into the water of the fountain and laughed—they were always laughing. And their mothers were so beautiful! Even the ones who were ugly or old. They all shone with happiness, as if they had absorbed something of their babies' glow. I took a piece of kaseri out of my pocket—I always craved that particular kind of cheese at precisely that hour of the day—and chewed it slowly. I let Lyn off her leash and she ran to play with the kids. I sat on a bench and watched. The mothers were exquisitely beautiful now that the sun was setting. Their eyes were fixed on their children, in case they fell or started quarrelling. A few of the kids were more lively than the rest. One fat little girl with a pink bow in her hair gave a sharp blow to a puny little boy with red hair and a freckled nose—and while his mother shouted at the fat girl's mother, who looked like an enormous velvet butterfly, the boy pushed himself between them and yelled:

—I want more! I want more punches!

Everyone in the park laughed, and I laughed too. I lit another cigarette and offered one to the woman sitting beside me on the bench. She looked at my belly and said:

—You really shouldn't be smoking. You've smoked a dozen cigarettes in the past half hour. Shouldn't you be thinking of your baby?

I was so ashamed that I got up and ran off. And I forgot to put Lyn back on her leash.

The second month of my pregnancy ended. I entered the third. At the end of the third month, I went back to the gynecologist.

—Where have you been? I was worried, he said.

—I want an abortion, I answered.

A deep silence fell in the office. My gynecologist, who was usually so friendly, looked at me coldly.

—Why do you want an abortion?

—Because I hate my husband, and I want to deny him the joy of having this baby.

I lit a cigarette.

—Smoking is not permitted in the office.

The gynecologist wouldn't even look at me. He

shuffled some papers on his desk. I kept smoking.

—Put out your cigarette at once. It's bad for the baby.

—But I don't want it, I don't want Alkis to be happy, I said, lighting another.

—What about you? Do you want it? The gynecologist looked me in the eye, suddenly sweet and tender. He reminded me of Aunt Louisa.

—Yes, I said, and started to cry, silently, but so hard that before long the front of my shirt was completely soaked, as if I had just taken it out of the washing machine. The doctor let me cry for a long time. My appointment had been for seven, but by now the sun was setting, so I must have been crying for at least an hour. The doctor switched on the light, a beautiful antique lamp that was sitting on his desk.

—You're entering your fourth month. He was speaking so softly that I had to lean forward to hear him.

—What you want is no longer just an abortion, at this point it's a surgical procedure.

I remembered my dream, the one in which I'd vomited up the baby and its velvety hands, and the office filled with the scent of jasmine.

—Be at the hospital at a quarter to eight tomorrow morning. Don't eat or drink anything prior to the appointment, not even a cup of coffee. We'll operate at nine, but there are some preparatory procedures. I'll give you my home number in case you change your mind during the night. We can cancel tomorrow's appointment at any point, it's quite simple. Your husband adores you. I remember the first time you came here together, he asked you to go outside so he could speak to me alone. "Doctor," he told me, "I don't want anything to happen to my wife. I adore her, and I know how much she wants this baby. And I want it, too. Because it'll be my wife all over again from the beginning, I'll get to experience her as a baby, as a child, a teenager, and I'll be so grateful. I hope it's a girl. I hope she has my wife's hair, and her laugh."

The operation took place the next morning. I stayed in the hospital for five days, in a room with two other women, both of whom had just given birth. The nurses would bring their babies in to be fed. I watched them insatiably. The smell of milk filled the room, the babies' mouths grasped the nipples like little suckers and drank greedily, their velvety hands resting on the white, swollen breasts. I lied to the two women, told them I'd had a miscarriage, so I could cry as much as I wanted. In the afternoon, during visiting hours, the room would fill with flowers, red roses, lilies, jasmine. Before that, around lunchtime, the three of us would watch *The Bold*

and the Beautiful on the TV in the room. I cried constantly. Through my tears I could make out hazy figures
moving on the screen, blondes in silk dresses who cried
and collapsed into one another's arms. The men all
wore suits and striped silk ties. After the show, we'd fall
asleep until late afternoon. I no longer dreamed.

They had Alkis come home from England.

—Your wife had a miscarriage, my gynecologist told
him over the phone.

The doctor came to see me, bringing a bouquet of
jasmine. He held my hand. We didn't speak. Then he
left, closing the door behind him carefully, like a thief.

Alkis brought me a huge bouquet of wildflowers,
which he knew were my favorite.

—I picked them myself, he said as soon as he
entered the room. I chose them for you one by one.

He didn't put them in a vase. He scattered them on
top of me, covering me in flowers from my feet to my
chest. He didn't say a word about the baby.

Does he know? I wondered. Alkis had an infallible
intuition, surely he knew. He kissed me on the mouth
and left.

—I'll come again at the same time tomorrow.

That evening, with the two women who had
become my friends, I watched a really great thriller on
TV. It was called *Dressed to Kill*.

41.

After the abortion, I returned home. It was autumn. Glyfada was ugly and melancholy. The clouds turned the sea in front of our terrace the color of ink, of dirty blue velvet. I dreamed of babies every night. Blond babies, dark-haired babies, boys, girls—in my dreams they all looked at me, crying.

—But *I* didn't kill you, I shouted at them in my dreams. It's Alkis's fault, he killed you, it was his sperm, I didn't want it inside me. It's Alkis's fault, Alkis's. Go be in his dreams, leave me alone.

In one of the dreams there was a baby who had Alkis's purple eyes. It was a boy. He flew around the bed holding a knife, then suddenly swooped down to attack me. The knife left a mark on my chest. I knew right away that this was the baby I had killed with the abortion.

—Why did you let them chop me up? he cried, flying around my face with dizzying speed, like a monstrous mosquito. He looked like a warrior, wielding the knife above his head. His eyes looked exactly like Alkis's, distant and metallic, only these purple eyes were filled with hate. He was pink and chubby, like an angel, unbelievably beautiful, which made the knife in his hand seem even more sinister.

—Why did you let them chop me up? he asked again. Why? I was a good baby and I really wanted to live.

—Babies don't talk, I told him bitterly.

—In dreams they do. He looked at me wildly. In dreams babies do whatever they want. When you kill a baby, it goes back to where it came from, a big room high up in the sky, with a view down onto earth. From up there they can see all the parents, and they pick which ones to go to.

—And you picked me?

—Yes. But when you kill a baby the way you did, it knows how to talk better than the others, because it learned to talk in its mother's belly. But instead of being born, it goes back up into the sky with a useless tongue, since it only has other babies to talk to, who don't understand anything. All you taught me was to cry and to curse. And now that I've gone back to the other babies, they won't play with me. They don't understand anything I say, but I have this wild look that makes them scared of me. Besides, I'm the only one who's ever come back after a willful murder—"abortion," I think they call it down there—and in the place where I am now, that's the ultimate sin and disgrace. The other babies still haven't gone down into the bellies of the mothers they chose, so they're fresh and pure, while I'm all butchered and polluted, blood still runs from my wounds, they still haven't healed. At the hospital when you spread your legs and they put you to sleep they chopped me up into pieces, and now my right arm is missing, I have to crawl around with just the left one and I'm always falling and hitting my head on the ground. And there are lots of babies ahead of me in line, it'll be ages before it's my turn to go back down. I'll be waiting for so long, with everything I learned on earth useless to me here. I'll be here for ages, all hacked up in pieces, waiting my turn.

Suddenly the room filled with babies flying around like bees. They whirled in circles over the bed with terrifying speed, while others poured in through the open window, pink and chubby as cherubs. But their eyes were wild, murderous. They carried chains, axes, clubs, and saws, and flew down on top of me and started beating me with their weapons.

—Now we'll kill you, we'll chop you to pieces, butcher you, like you did to our friend.

When the first club hit me and broke my nose and the blood began to flow, I let out a howl. I woke with a start and sat up in bed, bathed in sweat. I was trembling like a leaf.

Alkis awoke.

—Darling, what's wrong? You're drenched in sweat. You must've had another nightmare.

—Alkis, I said, Alkis, make love to me.

That night I conceived. While we made love, I pleaded for the same baby to return, the baby with Alkis's purple eyes, and the knife.

42.

Alkis made me go to a psychiatrist, because all day long I would shout:

—I hate you!

—And I adore you, Alkis would answer.

That was all we said to one another anymore, crying and shouting.

It was a Saturday, I think, when Alkis grabbed his head with both hands and started to cry like a child.

—If things keep up this way I'll go crazy, and you'll go on safe and unharmed as you always do, I'll go crazy, I can feel it, there's this humming in my ears like an earthquake is coming, and I keep seeing strange images as if I've taken some drug, I have to check a hundred times to make sure I've turned off the stove. Stop! Stop it right now!

I dressed very seductively for my first visit to the psychiatrist, in the black dress I'd worn to the casino with Vanessa. As soon as I put it on, it seemed as if ages had passed since that night. It had a high neckline and the back was open to the waist. I put on a pair of black high-heeled sandals that fastened with a thin strap around the ankle. I left my hair down. It had grown all the way down to my waist, but I pulled it over my shoulder, alongside my right cheek, so my bare back would show. I put on lots of makeup, something I never did, and got out my grandmother's old jewelry, a gold chain and a gold bracelet studded with diamonds. When I left the house at four that afternoon, passersby turned to stare at me, and one man whispered as he walked by, "You look like a Christmas tree. All that's missing is the lights."

I went into the office. The psychiatrist was smoking a pipe, and I was reminded of Vanessa and her slim tortoise-shell cigarette holder. I sat down in an armchair opposite him. A deep silence fell in the room. It was unbearably hot. The noise from the cicadas outside was deafening. I started rummaging around nervously in my purse.

—Feel free to smoke, the psychiatrist told me.

I lit a cigarette. A second silence, even longer than the first, made me start sweating, or maybe it was just the heat. Finally the psychiatrist switched on the fan that was sitting on his desk. The breeze sent all the smoke into my face. My eyes welled up and tears began to roll down my cheeks, my mascara and rouge ran and I started to cough.

—Could you maybe turn the fan toward you? I asked.

Soon I was soaked in sweat, my face a mess of melted makeup. I took an elastic band from my pocket and pulled my hair back, took a tissue and wiped off all the makeup. Right away I felt better, and sat more comfortably in the chair.

The psychiatrist smiled.

—You have lots of different brands of cigarettes in your purse.

—Yes, I answered. I like the variety.

—But it must be tiring, always having to choose which brand to smoke.

I'd never thought of that before.

—Now that you mention it, I told him, I realize that it really does exhaust me.

—Wouldn't it be better if you chose one brand and stuck with it?

—Yes, I answered.

That thought brought me a huge sense of relief. But the sweat was still pouring down my face, and I kept dabbing at it with a tissue. I was about to faint from the heat.

The psychiatrist smiled again, a warm, friendly smile.

—Why didn't you ask me to turn the fan toward the middle, so that we'd both have a little air? Is it necessary for either one of us to melt in this heat? Isn't there some middle ground?

—I don't know, I answered.

Again I felt nervous, embarrassed, as when we'd both fallen silent. The psychiatrist turned the fan toward the wall, and finally the office cooled down.

Now the psychiatrist was looking out the window. He seemed distracted. He was smoking his pipe. I lit another cigarette. There was another long silence. But this time I wasn't nervous. I relaxed, crossed my legs, and let my purse fall to the floor.

—What are you thinking about? he asked.

—How I forgot to walk my dog, Lyn, before I came.

—Why did you forget?

—I wanted to make myself look nice for you, so I didn't have time to take her out.

—So you didn't forget.

—No, I answered. I didn't have time. Like I just said.

—You said you'd forgotten.

—No, I said I didn't have time, I repeated stubbornly.

—And why did you want to make yourself look nice for me? So I would like you better, or to give you some advantage over me?

—So I wouldn't have to talk to you.

This came from me spontaneously, without any thought, and I relaxed even more.

—So you dressed as if putting on a suit of armor?

We both laughed.

—When you feel beautiful, does it protect you from getting close to others?

—I've never thought of it that way before, but now that you mention it, around the people I love and trust I never wear makeup or dress up, I just wear jeans, a t-shirt and tennis shoes.

—Perhaps now we can get down to business.

Again a deep silence fell.

—Did you really want the abortion?

I was taken aback.

—Have you ever seen a movie called *Kiss of the Spider Woman*? I asked him for no real reason, just to say something, anything, to avoid answering his question.

—What brought that particular movie to mind? Yes, I've seen it, it's a remarkable film. What do you think of when you hear the word "spider"?

—An insect that eats its own children.

—That is, a creature that kills its children by devouring them, like a cannibal.

I felt extremely uncomfortable when he said the words "devouring" and "cannibal."

—I feel uncomfortable, I told him.

—To swallow and digest your own flesh, which is what your child is—isn't that a kind of murder? Though in primitive societies, people often ate babies born with deformities, it was a ritual, there was nothing wrong with it. But you haven't answered my question. How do you feel about your recent abortion?

—I don't feel anything, I answered, and started to cry.

He handed me a few tissues from the box on his desk. I blew my nose noisily. This time the silence lasted a long time. I couldn't stop crying.

—Is there perhaps another reason why you're crying?

—Yes, I told him. I'm crying because I didn't take my dog Lyn for a walk before I came, and now she'll want to go to the bathroom and she'll have to hold it in. She's so clean, you know, she never goes inside the house, or even on the terrace.

—Would you like to leave now to go and walk your dog?

—Yes, I'd like that very much, but now I'm here and it's impossible. Besides, it's so hot. Even if I was at home I might not take her out, I might just wait until evening when it cools off.

—Would you like another dog?

—Yes. I saw a black cocker spaniel in the window of veterinarian's office, where one of my husband's colleagues works. He's so small and black, with little round black eyes that stare mournfully out at passersby. The other day I went and held him in my arms. He licked me on the nose right away.

—Tell me about your dog, Lyn. I can tell she occupies an important place in your life, perhaps even the most important.

He shifted in his seat.

—And you still haven't said anything about your husband.

—But we're talking about dogs, and I don't take my husband for a walk every morning so he can pee.

He didn't laugh. He didn't even look my way. He concentrated on cleaning his pipe, lit it again, then looked me straight in the eye.

—Just now you said, "I don't take my husband for a walk every morning so he can pee." That's the funniest thing I've heard all day, yet you'll have noticed that I didn't laugh, as I did earlier. Perhaps your secret desire is to put your husband on a leash and walk him every morning, as if he really were a dog? At any rate, that's what I understood you to mean, with what you just said.

I was angry.

—So you're suggesting that I'd like to put a leash around Alkis's neck and take him out to pee? You must be joking.

—You said it, not me. Listening to what you said, I sensed that what you really want is for your husband to be your slave, a slave who adores you, just as your dog Lyn does, as a dog adores its master, devoted until death.

Suddenly he laughed—a fresh, contagious laugh— and the atmosphere changed.

—Well, at least for today, it's a sign of progress that

you forgot to take Lyn on her walk—or, as you said, didn't have time to walk her because you wanted to make yourself look nice for me. This all happened because you were coming here. Today, at least, I seem to have come first. He laughed again. That is, today you forgot to take your husband for a walk. And I'd never say that if, deep down, you hadn't identified your husband with your dog Lyn.

—I want to buy that black cocker spaniel I saw in the window, I told him. He's very lively, so I'll name him Tramp.

—Why not? he said.

Again I was angry.

—I love my dogs more than I love my husband.

—Why? Because they obey you, and your husband doesn't?

—It's not that at all! Not at all! I cried.

Again there was a deep silence. I was trembling like a leaf.

—Why did you have the abortion when you love your dogs so much? You have a great deal of love inside of you. Wouldn't you have loved the baby even more?

I felt as if I were about to throw up, just as in the dream when I'd vomited the baby and the poor thing had grabbed me by the neck with its little hands. My throat closed up completely and I felt my body breaking open, as if I were giving birth that very instant. I doubled over.

—I hate my husband, I suddenly cried. I hate him without knowing why. I don't want our flesh to come together. I would have liked to have some stranger's baby, but his I would have killed with my own hands—which is exactly what I did. You know it wasn't a miscarriage, it was an abortion, an operation. I was in my fourth month but I insisted on an abortion, I chose to do it, because it would have been part of Alkis, too. I wanted to drive him to absolute despair, maybe even to suicide.

I started to sob and shout at the same time.

—I hate all men! I want to kill them all, to annihilate them. When I was little I would wait every Sunday for my father to come and take me on an outing. I would get dressed the night before and sleep in my good clothes so I'd be ready. I would put on my dress with the little pink flowers, my shiny black shoes with Mickey Mouse on the toes, and get my lunch box ready: two sandwiches and a chocolate bar with almonds.

At dawn I would be waiting at the window, holding my lunch box. I wanted so badly for him to come! On the phone the night before he'd sworn on my life, understand, on *my* life, that he would come no matter what, that nothing could stop him from coming.

"Sunshine," he would say, "be ready at nine tomorrow morning. I'm going to take you to the beach to go swimming. So don't forget your swimsuit. Bring the one I like, the purple one with the green flowers that I bought for you when you were two."

"But Dad, it doesn't fit me anymore. I'm seven now."

Every Saturday we would say those exact same words, like a ritual. In the end my father would always say, a little absentmindedly:

"I'll go right now and buy you a new swimsuit, and I'll bring it to you tomorrow. What color do you want?"

"This year I want a bikini, all one color," I would say.

"Okay, sunshine, tomorrow I'll bring you a fantastic bikini, I saw one the other day in a shop window. My beautiful baby will wear it tomorrow, and I'll admire her as she builds castles and digs moats in the sand."

My father never came, not a single Sunday. He never brought me a bikini. We never went to the beach. Every Sunday, after standing motionless at the window from morning until late at night, I would take off the dress with the pink flowers and the shoes with Mickey Mouse on the toes, put the sandwiches in the fridge, and eat the chocolate bar while reading Hector Malot's *Nobody's Boy*. Then I'd put on my white nightgown and get into bed, but I wouldn't sleep. I would try to understand why he hadn't come, when he'd sworn on my life that he would come, no matter what.

Maybe it's my fault? I'd ask myself. *Maybe I don't deserve his love?*

At school the next morning, after a sleepless night, I would have dark circles under my eyes, and sometimes I'd fall asleep at my desk.

But during recess I would describe each and every detail to the other kids, who listened entranced as I told them what a wonderful Sunday I had spent with my father. How he'd bought me a bikini, all one color, how we'd gone to the beach to go swimming, how I'd eaten five Chicago ice creams, and in the evening we went to see a movie with Danny Kaye.

"You're so lucky," my friend Eleni would say. "I had to stay inside and finish my homework."

"Yes," I would reply. "I'm very lucky to have a father like mine."

Suddenly I stopped talking. Again the room filled with silence.

—Why do you hate your husband? the psychiatrist asked.

—Because he's a man, I answered.

—We have to stop for today, the psychiatrist told me, rising to his feet. I'll see you next Thursday.

One of my heels broke in the street. I had to hobble

the rest of the way home. As I walked I said out loud, again and again:

—You'll pay for this, too, Alkis. You'll pay a high price for this broken heel.

43.

As soon as I left Alkis I started watching videos and eating. Day and night, now, I watch videos and eat.

Alkis calls every ten or twenty minutes, but I never pick up. Sometimes I listen to his messages, when I feel like taking a break from the movies. Alkis's desperate voice on the machine:

—Why aren't you picking up? I know you're there.

But how can I answer the phone, stuffed as I am with pizza, ice cream, spinach pies, cheese pies, chicken pies, sausage pies, apple pies, ham pies? Only once, I wasn't thinking and absentmindedly picked up the receiver.

—Leave me alone. I'm watching *Gone with the Wind*. You interrupted me right when Rhett Butler gives that never-ending kiss to Scarlett, holding her by the waist and bending her backward like a reed, almost to the ground. If you had kissed me that way I'd just have been bored, but in the movie it makes me cry.

I've been watching videos and eating for a month. I've gained twenty kilos. The first day, I just happened to rent a movie because I had nothing else to do after my dance class. I was on a diet then, nothing but mineral water and fruit. The movie was called *Love Me to Death*. The plot touched me deeply: a woman falls in love with a veterinarian who has cancer. Later on she discovers that she has cancer, too. They fall passionately in love and die in one another's arms.

What gorgeous kisses! I would pause the movie at the moment of the kiss and stare at those united lips for half an hour. On the frozen screen, the lovers seemed already dead.

The next morning I rented ten movies, all romances, and bought lots of fancy foods: lox, caviar, strawberries, avocados, filet mignon, Madeira sauce, and plenty of fresh shrimp. And a bottle of pink champagne. That first week I watched nothing but exquisite romances, full of love and kisses. And the foods I ate were exquisite, too. Before stretching out on the bed to begin the séance I would put on my best dress, by Yves Saint Laurent, and black high-heeled Rosseti sandals. I would make up my face lightly, pull a little table over to the bed, and place a silver case of Davidoff cigarettes beside the food. That first week I watched about ten movies a day, from four in the morning until evening, then fell asleep early, around nine.

I was so happy! The house filled with kisses, soft music, and words like, "Darling, I've found you again after so many years. I'll never let you leave again!"

Alkis called constantly.

—Darling, answer the phone, I know you're there.

I've thought it over. I don't want us to separate, I don't want you to leave again.

Alkis's messages seemed so boring compared to the endless kisses and tears in my movies. Even my TV seemed to be crying, I saw hot tears welling up and trickling down the screen, tears and saliva from the kisses and love-making.

I ate constantly. Exquisite flavors filled my mouth as I sipped champagne and watched the lovers in one movie after another, without even a break between them anymore. Where had I seen that kiss? The movies got confused in my mind, just like the tastes of the various foods. Avocados or shrimp? Strawberries or ice cream? I watched and ate insatiably. In one scene, in a room at the Ritz, a gentleman in a tuxedo gazes at a woman in an evening gown printed with black and purple flowers.

—I've wanted you for so long, he tells her. Now that your husband is dead, nothing can stand in our way.

—Yes, says the woman, yes.

He rips open her dress and kisses her naked breasts as the two of them tumble onto the green and gold carpet.

—You're so refined, yet so raw, he tells her later, putting on his pants.

—You're so smart, yet so stubborn, says Alkis, crying into the answering machine.

I fell asleep.

The next day I rented only horror films. I was tired of the fancy foods, so I bought pizza, spinach pies, cheese pies, sausage pies, ham pies, and nine éclairs. I didn't dress up or put on any makeup. I stayed in my nightgown. But I painted my fingernails and toenails a dark red. My nails were the same color as the blood that now flooded the screen, the blood that welled from the screen and spilled onto the floor.

I began watching movies night and day.

In *Dressed to Kill*, a psychotic psychiatrist dresses up as a woman and uses a silver-handled razor to kill one of his patients, because he's in love with her husband.

I eat constantly. The pizza is greasy, as hairy as a spider. I no longer sleep. I stare insatiably at the screen. Knifings, throats being slit, heads rolling over freshly polished parquet, bodies dangling from stalled elevators, a man falling from the twentieth floor of a New York skyscraper.

Underneath the red polish, my nails are now black. I don't smoke Davidoffs anymore, but a brand of filterless cigarettes that leave a bitter taste in my mouth.

The next day I rented only hard-core porn. I didn't buy anything new to eat, just ate the half-spoiled leftovers from the day before. On the screen penises move in and out of vaginas with demonic speed to the rhythm of African music. I listen to the grunts and sighs as I chew on a spoiled éclair. Enormous breasts, thighs, black garters, expressionless faces—the room filled with filth and sweat, and at last the tears began to flow down my cheeks.

A month later I'd lost all the weight I had gained, and started going to my dance classes again. But every night I went alone to the movies and watched kisses, love affairs, murders, naked bodies making love. I no longer ate at all. I was like an alcoholic who suddenly stops drinking—I felt the same sadness, the same exhaustion. I was thin again, and very beautiful, but there was something so melancholy in my gaze that the usher always avoided meeting my eye.

44.

Two years had passed since I'd divorced Alkis. I hadn't
seen him since; we hadn't even talked on the phone. I
left as soon as I realized I had conceived again, on that
night during the heat wave. One night, after two years
of complete silence, I called him up.

—How's Caesar? I asked.

—Fine. And Lyn?

—Fine. She's stretched out at my feet, sleeping with
her eyes open, remember?

—What made you call me tonight in particular,
after two years of silence? Alkis asked.

—Tonight I'm celebrating. I just finished a novel.
I've been working on it ever since we separated, after
the abortion, remember?

—You mean the miscarriage?

—No. It was an abortion, I just never told you.

There was a long silence.

—And you, you wrote a novel? Alkis laughed.

—Yes. Me. Why are you laughing?

—Because I never expected you to actually finish
anything. You were always leaving. I always picture you
with a suitcase in your hand. I can't picture you sitting
at a desk. I always see you in motion.

—Yes. But back then I was leaving you. Now who
would I be leaving? I have only myself to leave now, and

I do think about sometimes. As for the book, I started writing it as soon as we separated, the very next morning. These two years, I haven't even left the house.

—Have you found a title?

—Yes. *Rien ne va plus.*

—Like at the casino? he asked. Only you would come up with a title like that.

Again there was a long silence.

—It's not just the casino, it's how life works, too, I answered. When the croupier says *Rien ne va plus* in those gorgeous salons smothered in red velvet, with those glittering chandeliers and huge mirrors and ladies wearing long gossamer gowns so they won't get hot while they play, their fingers weighed down with diamonds, faces broken beneath façades of deftly applied makeup—those ladies of a certain age who keep asking for a light from young men who smoke only Les Must de Cartier, the same young men they'll later spend the night with for a hefty sum and some gift, a black lacquer Dupont lighter or a fat gold Cartier chain—isn't all that like life itself? The game, the cruelty of old age, the wheel that spins without mercy—and you never know where the ball will stop.

The moment the croupier says *Rien ne va plus*, absolute silence falls in the casino. The game becomes fate. Waiting for the wheel to stop, for the ball to come to rest on one of the numbers, you're imprisoned, unable to act. You can't put down any more chips, and you can't take back any of the ones you've bet—whereas just a second before the croupier's solemn pronouncement, you could still put millions into the game, or take back whatever you'd bet. But now the game is out of your hands. So, Alkis, doesn't the same thing often happen in real life, too?

As I talked to Alkis, I watched my dog Lyn. She was sleeping, as always, at my feet. She woke, yawned, and licked my left foot.

—You know, Alkis, in my novel I describe the life we lived together, only differently. Otherwise it wouldn't have been art. I changed our life a lot. I even switched the roles. In my book, you're the monster and I'm the angel. I'm not the demon you knew and loved.

I made you gay, too. You remember how fascinated I was always by gay men? And it strikes me as so funny, because you're the only straight man who ever loved me. All my friends were gay. But instead of choosing one of them to be the main character in my book, I chose you. It really excited me—in an artistic way, of course—to transform a straight man into a homosexual.

Just imagine, Alkis, at the end of my novel, *Rien ne va plus*, you commit suicide. As if you could ever kill yourself! It's unthinkable, for anyone who knows you in real life. And you do something unspeakable, something you yourself would never do: you come to see me and you make love to me on the very eve of your suicide, just a few hours before you die. It's as if I'm making love with a corpse.

You were always so good to me, so patient with me! Perhaps more than you should have been. That's why I made you a monster in my novel, and gay. Perhaps when we were living together I secretly wished you were both.

In my novel you torment me mercilessly. Perhaps I even wished for that while we were married.

Just imagine, at the beginning of the book, it's our wedding night, and after the ceremony and the reception, you make me go with you to a gay bar. That chapter is superb. I still have rice in my hair from the church. You start hitting on a kid who's sitting across from you, who isn't even good-looking. The next day he comes to our house and you make love. I watch. That day, in the book, it's snowing, it's February, and we're sure the boy won't show. The roads are impassable. We've just made love and are reading Proust, naked in bed.

Suddenly the doorbell rings. It's the boy. He wanted you so badly that he walked for hours in the snow. And you want me there while you make love—otherwise, you say, you'd be bored.

Imagine, Alkis, just imagine, that I could write such things about you, so utterly foreign to who you really are.

—Why are you telling me all of this now, after two years of silence? When for two years I've been leaving messages on your answering machine, and you never once called me back? Alkis asked.

—I told you, I just finished my book, and I wanted us to celebrate.

—When we were married, you never told me you went to the casino. That secret life of yours hurts me even now, after two years apart.

—It's not a big deal, I told him. Back then, I had lots of secrets from you. Big ones, little ones. I lied to you all the time. Every day I would tell you I was going for cigarettes, but I never did. Instead, I would go to a café and drink an espresso, alone.

I had another secret, too, that was much more serious: on Mondays, Wednesdays, and Fridays, when your practice was open late, we had agreed that I would go by myself to the movies, remember? Well, I never went to the movies. I had three lovers. I saw one on Mondays, another on Wednesdays, and the third on Fridays.

It was sort of like the movies, though: dark rooms. The men would turn on the lights after we made love, just like an intermission. And as with characters in movies, I would forget their faces as soon as I left. Afterward, outside, I would light my first cigarette, alone at last, and with such a sense of relief, like when you step out of the theater and find yourself in the street again. Though they did give me such pleasure, especially the one on Mondays. If I'm remembering correctly, he was blond and well built. Or was it the dark-haired one on Wednesdays? I don't remember. The only thing I remember with great precision, as if it were happening now, is that first cigarette, alone at last, as soon as I'd left the building. I never took the elevator, that's how much of a rush I was in. I would tumble down the stairs singing *La Traviata*, the cigarette and lighter in my hand, and would light up as soon as I stepped into the street. What pleasure, that first drag!

I think I went to those three lovers only so I could light that first cigarette as I was leaving. I'd finished with them, as if a movie had ended.

I heard a sob from the receiver.

—Alkis, don't cry, it wasn't anything serious, despite the pleasure they all gave me. I only did it in order to have a secret from you, a big secret. You loved me so much that you never let me keep anything to myself, not a single thought, a single act. There wasn't anything that was entirely mine. I could have snuck off and gone for ice cream instead. Though of course ice cream wouldn't have given me the same pleasure, that same great pleasure, so the secret wouldn't have been as important.

Besides, Alkis, it was all your fault. You wanted to know where I was every second of the day. You were always calling me at the apartment to make sure I hadn't gone out. Every morning you asked what my plans were for the day. And if I told you I was going to a girlfriend's house, you'd call to make sure I was there. Of course I'd told them all that when you called, they should say I'd just gone out for cigarettes. I never actually went to see any of them.

I told you more innocent lies, too. You might ask if I liked some vase in a shop window, and I'd say no, even if I liked it a lot.

I lied to you everywhere, constantly, from the first moment we met. Even at Aunt Louisa's, that first Saturday, I was lying when I told you I loved the estate, and Aunt Louisa and Uncle Miltos. I only loved the twenty-seven dogs—they were the ones I went for, the ones I wanted to see.

That first time, remember? When I told you the estate was a paradise on earth? I was lying then, too. I was bored out of my mind on those Saturdays, with the TV and the kids and Aunt Louisa's incessant prattle. I couldn't wait to get out of there. I never liked the idea of paradise anyway, it always seemed so boring.

Why did I tell so many lies? I don't know. I only enjoyed lying to you. To everyone else I always told the truth.

Perhaps it was because those lies gave life a phantasmagorical glow. I could turn each day into fireworks, shape it however I wanted, as if I were God. And the strange thing is that you actually liked it, you knew I was lying to you, you even knew about the lovers, but you never said anything because you were afraid I would leave again. Isn't that right, Alkis?

You liked that endless lie that glittered like a diamond, it was a gift I gave you every day. You knew, but you didn't dare say anything, and didn't dare transform the lie into something else, give it another dimension, the way I did.

To embellish reality with makeup, with silk and royal purple, isn't that what we all should be doing? Beneath the life we live every day the silk and the purple are hiding, waiting for us. A person just has to dare to throw off his everyday clothes, to rip them off and to put on the silk and purple that exist, I know it. But we're the ones who cover them up. Out of boredom, indifference, fear. Mostly fear.

So right from the first moment I met you, my lies were always the truth: in telling them I unveiled the world for you—the hidden world, the true world.

You were really the one who lied. You wanted everything to remain untouched, paradise to be paradise, and me an angel. But you made a fatal mistake: you never believed me. You never understood why I lied, that through my lies I was giving you a unique gift: the truth. You always tried to control me—out of love, of course. But is there any word more ambiguous than the word "love"?

Alkis, I would have preferred if you had loved me less and understood me more.

Alkis, true reality is liquid like a stream, pure and treacherous like a desert wind, real only when it's false.

My truth was always hiding behind those lies. But perhaps you didn't love me enough, or didn't have the imagination, madness, or balls to become an alchemist of life like I was, to spin gold out of the boredom and emptiness that surround us.

I would have loved you then, Alkis. How much I would have loved you if you had just said: "I know you don't go to the movies on Mondays, Wednesdays, and Fridays. And I think it's extraordinary how you transform your lovers into films, so it's just as if you really were going to the movies, and I'm not jealous at all. But don't you think, perhaps, that a good film is worth more than even three lovers?"

Or if you'd said: "Why don't we make love only with each other, since I know how much pleasure I give you, and afterward, every Monday, Wednesday, and Friday night, we'll go to the movies together, and choose the films carefully, as if they were your lovers, and we'll experience them together, in our minds, you and I."

How much I would have adored you, Alkis, if you'd said all that, how much I would have respected you, how much you would have excited me, body and soul!

But you never said anything. You knew, but didn't dare speak, because you were scared I might leave again—and you infected me with that fear, and that's why I left. You forced me to leave, you pushed me away.

I might be even more unhappy about our separation than you. Because I know why I left, while you never understood.

Alkis, I loved you. And you ruined everything by treating me like a liar. You were always checking up on me: where was I, who was I with, even who I was—I said, breaking into a laugh.

You know something, Alkis? Beneath all that cleverness, you're pretty stupid. Just like reality, which you always wanted to be static, your cleverness is false, a façade, a mask for your fear.

You know something, Alkis? I hate you. Because you're so good, and yet such a fool. You never understood anything about life. You had the audacity to think you could keep me close to you with your love.

Paradoxically, I'm the only woman who never really lied to you. I simply distorted reality in order to bring it closer to the truth. But you didn't understand anything. Anything. And I hate you for that.

You were the one who always lied, not me. You're the one who abandoned me. Me, I just left. So find another woman, a woman who will actually go to the salon every Monday, Wednesday, and Friday for her manicures and pedicures and waxings, and who'll lie to you constantly. You never understood me. And that's why you don't deserve me. But let's stay friends. After all, friends are people who don't really love one another. You only deserve my friendship. As for you, feel free to love me as much as you want. Since it's not really me you love, what do I care? You love a figment of your own imagination, a veterinarian's wife. That's all I wanted to say. Now I have to paint my nails and try out a new brand of cigarettes, Rothmans Reds. I'm dying to try them.

I heard him sobbing into the receiver.

—Alkis, don't cry. Do you want to come over and celebrate?

—Celebrate what? Alkis answered. We've been separated for two years, and I miss you more each day. Life
without you bores me to death. I'm with a woman now
who's very smart and very beautiful. We have great sex.
But she never says, "I'm going for cigarettes," and goes
for ice cream instead, the way you did. You—you would
disappear all of a sudden, and I never knew where you'd
gone. But with her, every Monday, Wednesday, and Friday when I stay late at the office she really does go to
the movies, not to any lovers. I always know where she
is, every minute of the day. As for the phone calls, she
beats me to it, she calls me at the office and says: "Alkis,
from three to a quarter to five I'll be at the salon,"
"Alkis, I'll be at the university from eight to nine"—
she's a professor of semiotics—"Alkis, I'll be home at
twenty to ten," "I love you, Alkis" I never call to check
up on her, because I know she's telling the truth. How
much I miss your lies! It hurts her that I never call. But
she always beats me to it, she doesn't leave me room to
worry, to doubt. With you, I'd chase after you all day,
I'd call everywhere and never find you. What pleasure!
Only now do I realize how much I enjoyed that con-
stant absence. You left me free to love you as much as I
wanted, and I adored you for it. Never to know where
you were—it brought tears to my eyes, tears of pain,
but tears of pleasure, too, of adoration. I still adore you,
my little Proust. You're such a child, and yet so cunning,

an angel and devil in one. I miss you so much, so much! Can I come over?

—Yes, I told him.

—I'm on my way. I've waited for this moment for two whole years.

He came with an enormous bouquet of chrysanthemums.

—But they're the flowers of the dead, I said.

He didn't answer.

We made love all night long. We'd never made love like that when we were married. We looked up at the full moon, and it looked down on us.

Afterward, Alkis stretched out naked on the bed and silently smoked a cigarillo, stroking my breast.

Day was breaking.

—I have to leave. I have to get ready for work. Will I see you again? he asked from the door.

—From now on, you'll be seeing me every day, I answered.

I heard his car disappearing around the corner.

It was dawn, but the moon was still in the sky. It seemed to be hanging by a golden thread that was about to break. The sky was dark blue, like ink.

I felt an indescribable pleasure, alone in the night. The city slept, sailing on like a ship. I went into the bathroom and washed the makeup from my face with Clinique Mild soap. The blue and purple eye shadow began to run, the black mascara, the rouge on my cheeks. I looked in the mirror. I looked like a clown. I patted some Clinique Clarifying Lotion No. 2 onto my face with a cotton ball, then put on my moisturizer, Dramatically Different Moisturizing Lotion. My face glowed, shining, translucent. For the first time I realized that I was much prettier without makeup. I slathered my whole body with Clinique Exfoliating Cream to take off the dead cells. My skin became as soft as a baby's. I brushed my hair a hundred times, fifty with my head bent forward and my hair touching the marble tiles, and fifty with it flipped back over my shoulders. I put on my white linen nightgown with lace at the shoulders and hem. Then I went out and sat at the round table next to the big window.

The moon was like mercury, the sky the color of some pale, metallic ink. The moon and the sky both seemed to have come right into the room, and the walls and ceiling glowed a frozen white.

I felt an indescribable pleasure, so intense that my legs trembled.

I put all the different brands of cigarettes I'd

collected over the years on the large round table. Then all my body and face creams. I carefully read the directions for each cream and the percentages of nicotine and tar on the bottom of every pack of cigarettes. I lined up the creams: Clinique, Lancôme, Vichy, Estée Lauder, Prairie, Chanel, Yves Saint Laurent, Clarins, Guerlain. Then I read the names of the cigarettes out loud, from the mildest to the strongest. I had a few brands of cigarillos, too, Silk Cut Yellows, Blues, and Purples, Les Must de Cartier, Trussardi Extra Mild. As I read the names of the strongest brands, my voice, too, acquired a new strength: Rothmans Blues, Rothmans International, Dunhill, Benson & Hedges, John Players in the flat black box, John Players in the white box with the blue sailor, gold-filtered Davidoffs. Then my voice was even stronger; I had reached the cigars: Café Crème, Partayas, Tobajara, Lonja, Rivarde.

There was one brand of cigarettes I'd never smoked before, Rothmans Reds. They had just come onto the market. I lit one ceremonially with my black lacquer Dupont lighter, a gift from Vanessa. The cigarette had an extraordinary taste, neither light nor heavy, and the smoke slid down my throat like velvet.

I put on some music, Billie Holiday.

Night and day…

Her voice flooded the room, climbed up the walls, spilled over the carpet, caressed me.

I smoked. I fixed a Bloody Mary and took it with me into the bathroom.

I poured bath oil into the tub and let the hot water run. Soon the bathroom had filled with steam.

With my finger I carefully wrote my name on the mirror, which had fogged over with fragrant mist: Louisa.

Suddenly I remembered Aunt Louisa, her lapdogs covering her like a fur coat as she came running into the yard to greet me.

I painted my nails a dark red.

45.

Louisa sank into the hot, fragrant water, still wearing her white linen nightgown.

In her right hand she held a scalpel she had stolen from Alkis's office years earlier, because the silver handle had caught her eye.

Once in the hot water, she was about to plunge the blade deep into her veins. But she felt such pleasure at the thought of it that she almost fainted. It was an image she had carried inside her for years. She would walk down the streets and see this image—the bathroom, the razor—reflected in all the shop windows, or, if it was raining, shining on the asphalt.

An orgasm began to tremble above her like a foreign body. It moved slowly from her chest down to the tips of her toes.

She smoked her Rothmans Reds and drank her Bloody Mary, her nails dark red against the glass. Her white linen nightgown swirled in the water. Her little dog Lyn came and stretched out on the marble tiles beside the tub.

The velvety, metallic voice of Billie Holiday came from the other room. The sun had begun to rise.

How beautiful life is! Louisa suddenly thought, as if waking from a dream.

She climbed out of the tub, tossing the scalpel across the room. Now Billie Holiday was singing, *I don't want to lose you…*

Louisa wiped the condensation from the mirror with a towel, erasing her name. Then she looked at herself. She was there, unharmed. She began to laugh, as if she had escaped from some childish prank she'd been about to play on herself. She was there, and her scrubbed face shone. Her laughter was fresh. She hadn't laughed like that since she was a little girl.

She dressed hurriedly. She turned off the record player and threw all the creams and cigarettes in the trash. She made the bed, which still smelled of Alkis.

—Alkis, darling… she whispered.

The room took on its customary appearance.

The sun shone in the sky. Its rays made the sea shimmer. A cool breeze was blowing. The heat wave had finally ended.

She went into the bedroom, quickly packed her bags, picked up her dog Lyn, and left the apartment, carefully closing the door behind her.

Louisa traveled for three days on the train, heading north. It began to get cold and to rain. After the heat wave, this sudden change of climate calmed her. She felt the skin all over her body begin to breathe again, and she often stuck her head out the window, letting the strong drops of rain hit her face. She barely smoked at all. She slept a lot, read, closed her eyes and dreamed, lulled by the rhythm of the train. For the first time in her life she was happy. She turned the pages of her book, or let it fall to her knees as she looked out at the scenery. She closed her eyes, lit a cigarette, listened to the fat raindrops hitting the window, put on a sweater, and fell asleep again with Lyn at her feet.

On the morning of the second day she awoke in a lush green landscape. She had never seen such tall trees, such thick foliage.

The train kept stopping at stations in the middle of nowhere. Even the houses were smothered in green leaves.

On the afternoon of the third day the train reached the sea.

The landscape changed. It was a sea she had never seen before. Huge waves crashed on the rocks, and green trees tumbled down the slope of the mountain, merging with the deep green of the sea.

It was cold and a fine rain was falling, coiling the landscape in mist, as if the mountain were exhaling vapor.

Louisa put on her raincoat and stepped from the train, carrying Lyn in her arms.

The hotel was high on the mountain. Far below, the big waves pounded rhythmically against the rocks. Her room had a view of the green mountain and, further down, the North Sea. A lighthouse flickered on and off in the waves.

Louisa opened the window. It had stopped raining but the sky was dark, like black ink. A storm was building. The clouds were so thick and low that Louisa tried to reach out a hand and catch them.

This green mountain reminded her of something, as did the approaching storm, the pitch-black sky.

—*La Tempesta*... she whispered. She remembered the painting by Giorgione at the Gallerie dell'Accademia in Venice, she remembered Vanessa, she remembered a different life.

Now the landscape gives off a sweet sense of anticipation—perhaps of rain. It exudes a silence, a calm. Louisa feels as if she has finally reached her destination, after years of wandering and pain.

The scenery she sees from the window is shady, full of green trees.

Louisa hears the rain falling suddenly, cataclysmically. She is filled with a sweet euphoria. She closes her eyes.

At last! She is alone! She stretches out on the bed and listens to the raindrops hitting the pane. She falls asleep with Lyn in her arms.

Louisa dreams that she's in Venice, standing before a painting at the Gallerie dell'Accademia. The painting is *La Tempesta*. In a landscape full of mystery, a thunderstorm is about to break. A woman, naked from the waist down and with one breast showing, is holding a baby in her arms as if about to nurse it. Opposite her, at the other edge of the painting, against a background of foliage, a man in breeches and a red waistcoat stands watching her. She's looking off, somewhere else. The man is carrying a staff. There is a sweet sense of anticipation—perhaps of approaching rain. There is a silence, a calm. The two figures have finally arrived at their destination, after ages of wandering and pain. The landscape is shady, full of green trees and white clouds with curves as round as a woman's breasts. Water gushes from a spring.

In her dream, Louisa is in the painting. She is lying in the shade of green foliage. A spring gushes beside her. She puts her hand into the cool water.

In this absolute silence, she falls asleep.

46.

Louisa's child lived on the estate with Aunt Louisa and Uncle Miltos.

He was now two years old. He had Alkis's purple eyes and Louisa's blond hair.

He was a happy baby. He played with the twenty-seven dogs, and at night when the parrot yelled "Down with the General!" he would dissolve into laughter. Everyone adored him.

And he loved them all, the people, the animals, the plants, all living things.

The child, they called him Alkis.

acknowledgments

Margarita Karapanou was thrilled when, last fall, the newly formed Clockroot Books decided to publish three of her novels in English translation. Her death in December 2008 was a shock and a sorrow, but it is a comfort to know how pleased she would be that English-language readers will now be able to enjoy her work as readers in Greece have for so long.

I started translating *Rien ne va plus* over ten years ago, when I was still a beginning student of Greek. It was one of the first Greek novels I read. It was, indeed, one of the books that taught me Greek—and while it may not have taught me to translate, it certainly made me feel a pressing desire to try. I had no idea at the time that it would turn out to be one of the most difficult books I could have chosen. Its simple language is deceptive; *Rien ne va plus is hard*. It's embarrassing and endearing, captivating and manipulative by turns. It demands things a reader may not always want to give.

So translating Karapanou's novel has been a challenge, and I am deeply grateful for the help I have received along the way. I am most indebted to Dimitri Gondicas, my teacher, mentor, and friend, who ten years ago sat with me and painstakingly went over my text word by word. In fact, every book I'll ever translate should be dedicated in part to Dimitri: he continually makes me feel the importance of sharing the books I love. I would also like to thank my parents, David and Helen Emmerich, and my brother, Michael Emmerich, who have offered corrections and suggestions on several versions over the years. Nicholas Salvato and Michael Sherry read and commented on the translation's earliest incarnation, and Patricia Akhimie did the same for a more recent one. Hilary Plum, my editor at Clockroot, has been wonderfully supportive and encouraging, and I am very grateful to her and to Pam Thompson for having faith that Karapanou's work will find the audience it deserves in English.

—Karen Emmerich